Raven

Book 2
Beauties with Blades

Laurel O'Donnell

Dearest Reader,

Thank you for reading Raven and Landyn's story, the second book in the Beauties With Blades™ series. Raven is such a strong character, and she is the only one who could endure the trials and tribulations in this story. It was exciting to watch her grow and fall in love.

Landyn is the one hero who could win Raven's heart. I hope you agree. And I hope you like their story as much as I enjoyed bringing it to you.

So please suspend your disbelief for a short while and join me on Raven's adventure.

Welcome to my world!

Laurel

The Hawkes

The Hawke sisters are far from typical women. Raised by their father the legendary John Hawke, the girls are taught how to fight with swords, how to survive in a man's world, and above all how to protect the family. They are Beauties with Blades.

Come along on their adventures as these bold and brave women save innocents, discover secrets, and fall in love.

PROLOGUE

England
1292

The sound of birds chirping floated in through the window of the one-room cottage. Even though sunlight streamed through the open shutters, the room was cold. The hearth against the far wall was out, the fire long since extinguished. The brightness of the sun and the happy song of the birds were strangely out of place.

Raven Hawke, a thin girl of eight summers, stood over the straw mattress tucked into the corner of her home, staring at her mother. Her mother's eyes were closed, her brown hair framed her head, and her hands were limp at her side. She had been motionless for a long time now.

Willow, the youngest sister, gently called out to their mother and shook her. But their mother did not move.

As the oldest, Raven was expected to be in charge. To know what to do. Yet, she couldn't move.

She silently begged her mother to get up, to breathe, but she had watched her mother for a long time, watched her chest for the rise and fall of her breathing. There was no movement. Still, she appeared to be sleeping. Raven anticipated that her mother would sit up and smile and hug them at any moment, even though she knew she would not.

Sage, the middle sister, sat in a rickety chair behind Raven at the table. She crossed her legs beneath her. Her brown hair fell in disarray about her shoulders as she pouted and flicked at a small indent in the wood of the table.

Willow knelt on the floor beside her mother's mattress. Her long, blonde locks draped over her mother's half-open hand. Reaching out, Willow pulled a ragged blanket over her mother to her chin before placing a tiny hand on her cheek. She turned her head to lock a watery gaze with Raven. "She's cold."

"She's dead," Sage proclaimed.

Raven spun, casting a harsh glare and reprimanding, "Sage!"

Sage uncrossed her legs and pushed herself from her seat. Her auburn hair was unkempt, hanging around her shoulders like an old cloak. Her eyes were aged, haunted past her six summers. "It's true! Mother's gone," she insisted.

Willow sobbed quietly, her small body shaking.

Raven glanced at her youngest sister before taking a step toward Sage with her fists clenched. Sage had always been like that—stating facts. This wasn't the time. They had to figure out what to do. "Look what you've done now!" She flicked a hand at Willow.

"She should know the truth," Sage said with a frown.

"Not like that. You don't even care that Mother is gone!" Raven accused.

Sage stuck her tongue out at Raven.

Raven nearly lunged to yank Sage's hair and hit her arm, but she felt a tugging at her skirt and paused, looking down.

Willow stared up at her with large, wet blue eyes. "What will we do without Mother?"

Sage stared at Raven with expectant eyes.

Raven was supposed to have all the answers. She was supposed to know what to do. She cast a look at their mother, at her gray skin, at her peaceful, sleeping face. Raven's shoulders slumped, and she wrapped her arms around her stomach. A frown formed on her brow. What were they supposed to do now? How could Mother do this? How could she leave them alone?

This time, Raven didn't have any answers.

Suddenly, the door flew open, sending a gust of air into the room.

Willow ducked behind Raven, hiding. Sage took a step back from the door, moving to her sister's side.

Raven lifted her chin to glare at the strange man standing in the doorway.

Silhouetted by the sunlight behind him, the tall man ducked beneath the doorway to enter the cottage. His severe gaze moved from sister to sister. His dark, shoulder-length black hair blew forward, pushed by a rush of wind curling into the room. His jaw was square and firm, and his eyes were hard. Leather armor fit snugly over his torso, and a sword was strapped to his waist.

Raven instinctively placed a protective arm around Willow, drawing the man's gaze. Her heart beat madly out of fear.

His stare shifted to their mother. His wrinkled brow softened, and the sternness in his face diminished. He strode across the room, striding past the girls until he was at her side.

He knelt at the woman's side and stared for a long moment. Easing a strand of brown hair from her forehead, he tucked it behind her ear. He touched her hand, squeezing it, before lifting the blanket over her face.

He stood, inhaled deeply, and turned to them.

Raven hugged Willow against her. She didn't know this man. She didn't know what he wanted or what he would do.

"Gather your belongings," the man commanded in a deep voice. "Only bring what you can carry."

Startled, Raven could only gape at him. She clutched Willow tightly. It wasn't the man's appearance that sent shivers racing down her spine. It was his voice. Serious, forceful.

It was familiar.

"Who are you?" Willow asked in a timid voice.

He approached, his boots thundering on the wooden floor.

Raven retreated, pulling Willow with her.

Sage peered around Raven's shoulder.

Raven lifted her chin higher. She would not let him hurt her sisters.

The man stopped before her, and she met his stare.

Dark eyes swept her, assessing. "I'm your father."

CHAPTER ONE

France
October 6, 1307

"No. Absolutely not," Raven Hawke said, crossing her arms.

Moonlight shone down on the three sisters in the dirt yard behind the wooden inn. A horse whinnied from the stables across from the building.

Raven glared at Sage. Her sister was gently biting her lip, pleadingly clutching a black book against her leather-armored chest. A lock of her brown hair fell over her forehead, freeing itself from the braid she wore.

Willow stood beside Sage, her hands clasped as if in prayer. Her blonde hair glimmered in the moon's light, and her blue eyes sparkled. Even her wide-eyed look could not budge Raven's decision.

Raven couldn't believe Sage and Willow had come to her seriously, suggesting they defy their father's orders. His instruction was for them to go to Sybil's farm and wait for him. And now, Sage wanted to travel a half day's ride to the Chateau le Bezu because of a *book*. Her sister was brilliant, but right now, addle-brained.

"Father wouldn't want us traveling the roads without him." Raven walked across the yard toward the stables. She couldn't believe Sage had mentioned disobeying Father's order. What was she thinking? They needed to be on the road to get to Sybil's farm.

Sage and Willow stood unmoving. They cast glances at each other.

"He doesn't have to know," Willow pleaded, trailing Raven. Sage followed, holding that black book to her chest as if it were the most precious treasure in the realm.

Raven whirled on Willow. "Don't you think Sybil will tell him we didn't help her with the harvest and we weren't around for an entire day?"

Willow cast an imploring glance at Sage for help.

"We'll make something up," Sage told her. "That we were out hunting."

"All day?" Raven asked in disbelief. She was an excellent hunter. It only took her half a day to return with an animal. She put a hand on her hip. "And what do we say when we come back with nothing?"

"We didn't find anything," Willow added to the story.

Raven's lips quirked in skepticism. "And you think Father will believe that?"

"We got distracted practicing," Sage suggested quickly.

Raven glanced at Sage. Her brown eyes were wide and bright with hope.

Sage was smart. Practicing was the only thing

that would pacify their father. Working on their skills was the only excuse he would understand.

Willow nodded enthusiastically, a curl of blonde bobbing with the movement. A grin spread over her face. "We could stay an extra day and help Sybil with the harvest. It will work! Please, Raven."

Raven shook her head in doubt. Now they were considering *lying* to Father. What if he found out? They would be in even more trouble. And all that trouble wasn't worth it just for some old monk to read a book. She could understand Sage's interest in the book; Sage always asked for someone to teach her to read. But Willow didn't care for books. That realization made Raven pause. She swiveled her glare to her youngest sister.

Willow's hands were clasped beneath her chin.

"Why is this so important to you?" Raven demanded. She jerked her chin at Sage. "I can see Sage being so adamant, but you? You want us to ride an entire day for some old monk to read a book? You've never cared about a book before. What do you think it's going to say?"

"I don't know," Willow admitted. "But aren't you curious?"

"No," Raven insisted. "I don't care about a book. I'd rather be practicing. Or doing something that will help me hone my skills. And you should, too." She looked at Sage. "*Both* of you."

Sage scowled. "Books are important," she insisted.

Nothing new there, Raven thought. Sage always thought books were worth more than gold.

"They hold knowledge, and knowledge is power," Sage continued.

"I don't want that kind of power," Raven replied. "It's dangerous."

"That's Father talking." Sage lifted her chin and ran a hand over the black leather of the book tenderly. "I want to know what it says. And I'm going to le Bezu whether you come or not."

Willow gaped in disbelief.

Raven's mouth dropped in shock for a moment, and then she snapped it shut. Her lips thinned, and her eyes narrowed. "I'll tell Father."

"I don't care. I'm going." Sage brushed past Raven and marched toward the stables. "You do what you have to."

Raven stared, stunned. Sage had never defied father's order before. Their father had told them to head to Sybil's farm and help with the harvest until he returned. Her fists tightened as her shock slowly gave way to anger. Father would not be pleased. She worked hard to follow her father's rules, to follow his orders, to please him. And now, Sage was going to defy him. Yet, Raven knew her father would be even angrier if she let Sage go the chateau alone. He always told them to stay together, that there was safety in numbers.

Willow stood for a long moment, staring at Raven. Then, she hurried after Sage.

Raven cursed quietly. She couldn't let them go without her. The Chateau le Bezu was half a day's ride. Those two could get hurt if they went alone. And she would be responsible. She closed her eyes in frustration. She didn't want them harmed. It was her job to protect them, to make sure they didn't do something reckless. With a sigh of resignation, she followed them into the stables. "This is not a good idea."

Each woman moved to the stall where their horse was stabled.

Willow's voice floated to Raven over the side of the stall. "When has anything worthwhile been a good idea?"

Raven shook her head. She didn't think this was worthwhile. Father was going to be furious when he found out.

They had been riding for most of the night. Raven knew Sage must be excited to have a book read to her because it was the one thing she was passionate about. Reading. Books. Knowledge. Raven rolled her eyes. The only knowledge they needed was how to be better with a weapon to defend themselves and their family. She clenched her fists over the reins. A book. What a waste of time. All one needed was a sword. Raven followed Sage down the road, keeping her doubts and complaints to herself.

Thunder was breathing hard, and Raven knew her horse was becoming tired. It was a long trip for him. "We should rest," Raven called.

Reluctantly, Sage agreed. She led them to the side of the road, where a hill rose to their right, and flat land stretched to their left.

Raven scanned the area. It was a suitable spot to stop. No hiding place for brigands or robbers.

They dismounted, and all the women immediately saw to the needs of their horses. Raven checked her steed's reins and bridles. When she was finished, she patted his neck and bent over to stretch out her sore leg and back muscles. It was a long trip for her, too. It was a long trip for all of them.

Willow stretched her back, twisting it from side to side before heading off the road, where she sat down in a grassy area. She reached into her armor and pulled the black book out. They kept valuable items with them, not in saddle bags. It was safer that way in case they were robbed.

Raven wondered what made this book so valuable, especially to Willow. She had never shown this much interest in a book before. There was something suspicious about it.

Sage joined Willow, sitting beside her. Her shoulder bumped Willow's playfully. "Trying to read it?" she teased.

"I think I'll leave that to Brother Nicolas. Or you," Willow replied. "You've always wanted to read."

Raven shook her head in disapproval.

Sage sighed. "I wish someone would teach me."

Willow nodded and continued to turn the pages.

"Does it have pictures?" Raven asked, joining them. She glanced down over Willow's shoulder at the parchment pages of the book. The moonlight illuminated the foreign symbols. It would take valuable time to learn to read them. Time better spent working on skills they could use. She crossed her arms.

"No," Sage answered. "That's why we're taking it to Brother Nicolas. He can read it."

"What do you expect to find?"

Sage shrugged.

"The secret to the universe?" Raven mocked. "The fountain of youth?"

Sage rose quickly, annoyed. "You know, it's not always about gold and riches. What if it tells you a secret fighting method? A forgotten way to fight and win."

"What would I do with that? I already know how to fight."

"You can always be better," Sage snapped and stalked to her horse.

Raven shook her head as she watched Sage walk away. She turned back to Willow.

Willow eased the book closed and tucked it away into a pouch, tying it to her belt. "She likes books." She stood to face Raven. "And if it's important to Sage, it should be important to you, too."

Raven sighed. Willow was right. "It is. Except that if Father finds out what we're doing, he's going to be angry. And that's more important to me."

They arrived at the chateau by mid-morning and were escorted to Brother Nicolas in the catacombs of the keep. Raven vaguely remembered being here a long time ago. She recalled walking through hallways made of stone. Now, the hallways didn't seem as tall.

Brother Nicolas sat behind a wooden desk with books stacked on both sides. He was hunched over one book and looked up when they entered. The escorting monk announced the Hawke girls and cast them an annoyed look before departing. Brother

Nicolas was old, with hardly any hair on his head. The skin on his face was weathered and wrinkled. His back was arched beneath the brown monk's robe he wore.

As they entered his chambers, he rose slowly and crossed the room to greet each of them with hearty embraces, as if they were longtime friends.

Raven half-heartedly returned the hug. She didn't remember him, and his touch was uncomfortable for her.

When he finished hugging Sage, he clung to her, using her shoulder as a brace to return to his chair behind the desk. He sat down with a heavy sigh.

His blue eyes were wise, and intelligence shone from them. The corners of his lips had deep laughter lines. His skin sagged around his chin and strands of long white hair popped up from an otherwise smooth head. "It's so good to see you girls, although I never would have recognized you."

Willow smiled warmly at Brother Nicolas. She was the most social of them, and a simple glance could have men telling her what she wanted to know. Raven often wondered how she did it.

"You were this big," he held out a hand three feet from the floor, "when I last saw you three. And you were a rambunctious lot!" He chuckled deeply.

"How long ago was that?" Willow asked.

He pursed his lips in thought. "Neigh on twelve summers."

"Twelve?" Willow gasped.

Shortly after Mother died, Raven realized. Yes, that would make sense why she only vaguely remembered the chateau. It was long ago.

Brother Nicolas nodded. "Of course, you came back for visits. But not often." He gazed at Willow through narrowed eyes of thought. "You must be Willow."

Willow nodded, pleased.

He laughed and swatted his knee. "I remember those golden ringlets. Cried all night for your father. We didn't know what to do with you! You drove Brother Peter mad."

"She still drives some people mad," Raven muttered.

"I'm so pleased you came to visit again," Brother Nicolas said.

Raven sucked in her lower lip anxiously and looked at Willow.

"Well, actually, we came to ask a favor of you." Willow untied the pouch to remove the book. "We would like you to read this to us." She handed him the book.

Brother Nicolas took the book, angling it toward the light of the torch ensconced on the wall. He opened it and scanned the parchment pages. "Where did you get this?" The merriment left his voice.

Tingles of trepidation spread across Raven's shoulders.

"It was a gift," Willow explained.

"A gift?" Raven echoed as surprise washed over her. Sage and Willow had lied to her! They'd said Willow *found* the book. Who had given it to her?

Sage stepped up to the desk anxiously.

"Hmmm." He looked at the first page, leaning forward until his nose all but touched the parchment. A deep frown etched into his weathered forehead. He straightened and shifted his gaze to them. "Who gave you this book, child?" he asked in an almost whisper.

"A man," Willow answered evasively.

Raven rolled her eyes and shook her head. Men always bestowed presents upon Willow. That didn't ease her growing anger.

"Leave this book with me. No good will befall you if you keep it."

Raven scowled at the warning. What was in the book to elicit such alarm? Now she was interested.

Willow wondered, "Why do you say that?"

He pointed one of his crooked fingers at the first page, moving from one figure in the text to another. "I've been around for far too long. I've seen every kind of book there is. You can't read this. It is babble."

"Babble?" Sage echoed, frowning in confusion. "Why would someone write a book that you can't read?"

"Oh, you can read it. After you figure out the code."

"Code?" Sage glanced at the book on the desk hungrily.

Raven stiffened. Oh, no. Code. A mystery. Sage loved mysteries. Dread welled within her. She had seen that hungry look on Sage's face earlier.

"It has a hidden code," Brother Nicolas clarified.

"A hidden code?" Raven echoed, anxiety swelling inside her.

Sage leaned forward, eager. "Can you decipher it?"

"It will take time," Brother Nicolas admitted.

"But I can decipher it."

"Can you teach me?"

"Sage!" Raven objected. "We don't have that much time." They had to leave for Sybil's farm. She couldn't stay with Brother Nicolas and play these games.

"I would love to teach you," Brother Nicolas said enthusiastically. "It gets lonely down here. I would enjoy the company."

"Sage," Raven said between clenched teeth. "Can I talk to you?"

Sage glanced at Raven and then back at the book before moving away from the desk into a corner.

Raven followed her; her jaw clenched tight. She glanced back at Brother Nicolas and then at Sage, whispering, "You can't stay."

"I want to learn," Sage said in a quiet voice.

"The only reason I came is that you said we'd be back at Sybil's farm before Father arrived."

Sage shook her head and glanced at Raven. "You came because we are family."

"Which is even more reason for you to come back with us!"

"This is what I've always wanted. To learn. Brother Nicolas can teach me to read. To decipher the hidden code. How can I leave? How can you ask me to?"

Raven clenched her teeth, her brow furrowing. She didn't approve. Not in the least. Even though she was so angry with the entire situation, she knew Sage was right. Sage had always wanted to learn to read and now Brother Nicolas had said he would teach her. How could she deny her sister this opportunity?

While she didn't agree with her about many things, Raven loved Sage. Even if she insisted Sage leave with them, she knew Sage wouldn't. She knew this was what Sage had always wanted.

"Tell Father I left on my own accord."

Raven scoffed. "He will never believe that. He knows we would never let you go alone."

Sage sighed softly. "Fine. Then go and get him. Bring him back here. I will talk to him when he arrives. I will take full responsibility."

"Sage—" Raven protested weakly.

"I'm not leaving, Raven." She spun and walked back to Brother Nicolas and Willow.

Raven stood still for a long moment. She didn't like Sage's new defiance. Her independence. Still, she was torn. Their father would not be happy. She didn't want Sage to get into trouble, but Raven knew that somehow their father would blame her. She was supposed to be able to influence her sisters. And usually, she could. She sighed softly. How could Sage put her in this predicament? She closed her eyes and rubbed her forehead. This would not end well.

She whirled and followed Sage, announcing, "Sage is staying to help Brother Nicolas."

Willow gaped.

"Father won't mind," Sage reassured Brother Nicolas.

Raven knew she was lying.

"Brother Nicolas is a friend," Sage added, as if to pacify them.

"Willow and I will wait for Father's return at Sybil's farm," Raven explained, trying to get control of a rapidly spiraling situation. "We'll bring him back here."

"Bring him back?" Brother Nicolas echoed in confusion. "There's no need to bring him back. He is already here!"

CHAPTER TWO

Raven followed a short, young monk down the hallway to meet her father. Willow walked behind her. Sage had stayed with Brother Nicolas. The monk leading them wore a brown robe that reached to the floor and swooshed with each one of his small steps.

Raven was stunned her father was in the chateau. He had told them he was working a job. While he rarely provided more details, she'd assumed he was helping a villager or hiring his sword out to a nearby lord. While she was shocked, it didn't help ease her reluctance to see him. What was she going to tell him? They had purposely defied his order. Anxiety settled over her like a storm cloud.

The stone hallway was as cold as she felt inside. With each step, she attempted to formulate an excuse. She could blame it all on Sage, which would be the truth. But she knew her father would not accept that reasoning. She was the one he left in charge. She was the one her sisters were supposed to follow.

Raven searched the stone walls they passed as if they held the answer.

But only questions came to mind. Why was Father *here*?

They turned a corner and continued down another hallway. A stone corridor dotted with wooden doors stretched before them.

A moment later, she realized one set of footsteps was missing. She cast a glance over her shoulder and found her sister was no longer following.

Raven stopped. "Willow?" she called, perplexed. She glanced at the surrounding doors, but they were all closed.

"This way," the monk insisted quietly.

Raven hesitated, scanning the hallway. Where had Willow gone? "Willow?" she called again, her voice echoing through the corridor. She retraced their steps and peered around the corner, but the hallway was empty.

"Your father is this way," the monk said with a hint of impatience.

Raven glared at him in annoyance. Could he not see Willow was gone?

His eyebrow rose imperiously.

Raven tapped her lower lip. Something must have caught Willow's attention. Perhaps a hound to pet or...Raven thought feverishly...or a child to speak with. She clenched her lips. It was all too much to deal with. She'd speak with her father first. Together, they could find Willow. She might have gone back to be with Sage. Willow was certainly in the chateau somewhere.

With a sigh of resolution, Raven continued after the monk.

They turned another corner. Two more monks, wearing the same brown robes, passed them. They cast her a glance but moved on.

Finally, the monk she followed stopped at a wooden door. He paused to look back at her and then knocked.

After a moment, a man opened the door. He was tall, with black hair falling over his shoulders in waves. He had a square, clean-shaven chin; sharp black eyes that seemed to see everything; a straight, proud nose. He wore a black tunic that opened in a *v* at the front. "We asked not to be disturbed," he said in a harsh voice.

"My apologies, but Hawke has a visitor," the monk explained.

The man's dark eyes shifted to Raven and swept over her with a summative glance. A shiver coursed through Raven.

She immediately dismissed her reaction as irritation and her lips twisted in annoyance. "I'm his daughter," she stated, tilting her head and putting her hands on her hips.

The door flew the rest of the way open. Her father's imposing figure filled the frame. His dark hair was tied back from his face and his brown eyes were wide with surprise. Slowly, the shock drained from his face and a scowl of anger replaced it. "Raven."

She swallowed and dropped her arms. Oh, she was in trouble. And without her sisters to back her up. She prepared to confront his wrath alone. She took a deep breath and greeted him. "Father."

"Where are your sisters?" he demanded, looking down the hallway beyond her.

"They are here, in the chateau."

His gaze settled on her again and he swung the door wide to allow her entry. He closed it right behind her, shutting out the monk. "What are you doing here?" he demanded, his stern glare fixed on her. "You were to go to Sybil's farm."

She had practiced what she would say to him in her mind on the walk through the hallways, but now faced with his disapproval and anger, she floundered. She had to tell him the truth. "Willow found a book. Sage wanted to have someone read it. She insisted on coming to the chateau."

Her father's dark brow lowered farther. "And you allowed them to come here?"

Allowed? she thought. She hardly allowed them to come. Taking a breath, she acknowledged that regardless of what she told him, it would be her fault. She was the leader. She lifted her chin. "They were going to go without me. I couldn't let them do that."

"Where are they? Why aren't they with you?"

"They're in the chateau. Sage is with Brother Nicolas. Willow is here." She left out *somewhere*. "They are safe."

Her father exchanged a cautious look with the other man in the black tunic, and she paused.

Raven didn't like the look. She frowned. Something was going on. "They are safe here, aren't they?"

Her father's lips tightened.

"There is no time. We must leave," the man in the black tunic said.

Raven faced him, her hands on her hips defiantly. "We are not leaving without my sisters." Who was this irritating man? Her father would back her up. Family was the most important thing. He'd always told them that. She waited…

And waited. But her father remained quiet, and Raven finally turned to him.

He stood stoically, silent. His gaze focused intently on the other man.

"Father?" she called in disbelief.

He stared hard at the man. A muscle in his cheek clenched. "I'll take the men and leave. You help Raven find my daughters."

Raven's mouth dropped and she cast the man a look of disbelief. He wore the same expression as she did. "I don't need him. I can find them alone."

"John," the man protested.

Her father's lips flattened in displeasure. "When you find your sisters, you will go to Sybil's farm and wait for me there."

Her teeth ground. "I don't need—"

He ignored her, turning to the dark-haired man, who shook his head. "You will accompany her and help her find Willow and Sage. Once the girls are safely out of the chateau, you can join us."

"John—" he began to argue.

Her father's firm glance swung from the man to her and back. "Is that understood?" His voice boomed.

Raven had heard that tone before. It was stern, tinged with anger. That tone allowed no argument. She bobbed her head and looked down. "Yes,

Father."

"Yes, John," the man answered.

Her father put a hand on the man's shoulder. "See them to safety, Landyn."

Raven scowled at the faith and friendship her father clearly had with this man. He was as tall as her father with dark hair that hung to his shoulders. There was a connection between them, one that instantly filled Raven with longing and envy. She had always wanted her father's trust and respect. But he continued to treat her as a child. With that thought came resentment for Landyn. Who was he and how had he earned her father's respect?

Landyn nodded.

Her father turned to her with a forceful stare. "This is Landyn of Winchester," he told her. "I trust him completely. You will trust him also."

She glanced at Landyn. He stared pensively at her with dark eyes. Her gaze traveled over him. His tunic clung to his shoulders and biceps, and his muscles were outlined beneath. His torso thinned at his belt where a sword was strapped about his waist. He was not a monk.

Her father took a deep breath and brushed between them, marching down the hallway.

Raven watched his retreating back, disappointment churning in her stomach. "Father!" she called.

He paused and turned to her.

She hurried after him and stopped before him. "Where are you going?"

"I have a job to complete," he said in a gruff, exasperated voice.

She wanted to explain. She wanted to

apologize. But nothing she said would be enough for him. She had disobeyed his order. She nodded glumly but didn't move.

"Is there something else?" he demanded impatiently.

Her throat closed. *Yes! Put your hand on my shoulder.* She shook her head. "Be careful."

As he strolled away, she watched him for a moment. For years, she'd longed for nothing other than for him to see her as more than a child, as more than someone that needed to be protected. But it was to no avail.

Finally, she looked at Landyn and found him gazing at her with judgmental eyes. She lifted her chin defiantly. "I can find my sisters. I don't need your help. Good day." She started down the corridor, back the way she had come. She examined each room, searching for Willow.

"I'm certain you can," Landyn agreed, following her. "But John gave me an order. One I plan to see to completion." He trailed her. "Are you looking for someone?"

She didn't pause, continuing to glance into open rooms. "My sisters," she replied with disdain.

"You said one of them was with Brother Nicolas."

"Aye," she said curtly.

"Where is the other?"

"In the chateau," Raven said and paused at a juncture.

An armored knight with a red cross on his white tunic passed her down the intersecting hallway.

She glanced this and that but couldn't remember which way the monk had led her. All the stone hallways looked the same. She started down one of the corridors, continuing her search.

"Where in the chateau?" Landyn asked.

"If I knew that, I wouldn't have to find her."

"We can have the le Bezu monks look for her," Landyn offered. "And get the sister that is with Brother Nicolas."

Raven stopped and turned to him. "I don't need your help," she said firmly.

"You do," he insisted. "Or you would know where your sisters were."

She stared into his black eyes as she balled her fists at her sides. She didn't know what her father saw in him. He was annoying. Commanding. Domineering.

"Your father gave me an order," he reiterated. "Unlike you, I will do as told." He brushed past her.

Raven's mouth dropped open. The insult rankled her. She snapped her jaw closed and gritted her teeth as she watched him stalk down the corridor. She took up step behind him and her eyes burned into his broad-shouldered back.

He paused to speak with a monk with a shaved head. "We are looking for two women. The Hawke sisters. Have you seen them?"

"No," the monk replied.

"We need to find them."

Raven stepped up to his side. "Can you bring us to Brother Nicolas?" she interrupted.

The monk's gaze scanned her imperiously. He looked askance at Landyn, who nodded.

Adding insult to injury. Why did the monk seek Landyn's approval for her request? If Raven kept grinding her teeth, she knew she would have none left.

"This way," the monk said, leading them down the corridor.

Raven glared furiously at the two men walking before her. Then she shook herself. It didn't matter. The only thing that mattered was finding her sisters and making sure they were safe. Willow had to be here somewhere. Raven glanced into a room with an open door, but the room was empty. She tried to occupy her mind, but her rage wouldn't abate at being treated so poorly. It burned in her like a scorching fire.

They passed another doorway, and she peered in. Templar knights, wearing their familiar white tunic adorned with a red cross, sat around a large table. One man rose to close the door as if she were spying on them. She grimaced in distaste.

Chateau le Bezu was a Templar stronghold, but the amount of Templars present seemed excessive. She glanced over her shoulder to see white tunicked Templar Knights emerging quietly from some rooms and heading away from her. She paused, staring as they rounded the corner she had come from, walking in the direction her father had gone. So many knights moving in one direction. It was strange.

She watched until they disappeared around the corner. Where were they going and for what purpose? Curiosity itched inside her, but she had to find her sisters. She hurried after the monk and Landyn.

The monk led them through the stone corridors and down a set of stairs.

She recognized these steps, recalling the feeling

of dawn. She and Willow had ascended these stairs to locate their father and she remembered how, when they were climbing, the darkness had given way to a lighted corridor. Now it was reversed. She was descending into the dark, and only occasional torches in sconces lit the spiral stairs. The catacombs of the chateau stretched before her. The corridors were dank and musky, carved from the very ground around them.

She remembered these rooms and knew which one was Brother Nicolas's. She pushed her way between Landyn and the monk to hurry forward. The sooner she got Sage, the quicker they could locate Willow.

She entered the room and stopped, frozen. A sweet metallic scent Raven recognized immediately as blood filled the chamber.

Brother Nicolas sat in a chair behind the desk. His head was bowed to his chest. An arm was wrapped around his stomach.

She scanned the room for Sage, but no one else was there. She hurried toward Brother Nicolas as Landyn and the monk entered. If it weren't for the potent smell of blood, she would have thought he was asleep. When she came around the desk, she saw his bloodied hand resting across his stomach and a stain of red marring his brown robe, dripping onto the floor. She knelt at his side. "Brother Nicolas?"

His eyes remained closed.

She put a hand on his shoulder and gently shook him. When there was no response, she slowly stood, her gaze shifting to the pool of red below his chair. He was gone.

The monk hurried to Brother Nicolas's side, pushing her away.

She stepped back, allowing the monk to minister to Brother Nicolas. The monk placed his hand before Brother Nicolas's mouth to see if he was breathing.

Raven looked around the room. If Brother Nicolas had been killed, what happened to Sage? Her sister would not have allowed this to happen. "We have to find my sister."

"Your sister killed him," the monk accused.

Rage flared through Raven, and she straightened, facing him. "My sister would not kill an innocent man. It is not the Hawke way."

The monk retreated from her, glancing at Landyn. "She was the only one with him," he said weakly.

"We don't know that," Landyn said firmly.

"Someone else must have joined them. Sage would never hurt him," Raven insisted.

"Then why isn't she here?" the monk asked. "Where is she?"

Raven didn't have the answer. She twisted a lock of hair. Concern flooded her mind. Was Sage hurt? She regretted ever coming to the chateau. Especially over some damned book.

The book!

She scanned the desk and noticed the black leather book was not there. Had Sage taken it somewhere? Had Sage been here when Brother Nicolas was attacked?

"We should find your other sister," Landyn said. "Maybe they are together." He glanced at the monk. "See to Brother Nicolas."

The monk nodded.

Raven's gaze moved slowly over Brother Nicolas. Killed. By the looks of it, from a sword wound. But why? Who would kill a defenseless monk? What threat could he have posed? Tingles of forewarning danced across her nape. She had to find her sisters.

CHAPTER THREE

Landyn led the way through the hallway. He had spoken to numerous monks and while many were searching for the other Hawke sisters, the women remained missing. He had doubts whether they were still in the chateau. But he had no time to figure out this puzzle. He should be at John's side, leading the caravan.

He glanced at the woman beside him. She wore a concerned frown on her brow. And what was he to do with Raven?

"Their horses!" Raven exclaimed.

Landyn stopped and looked at her, scowling in confusion.

"They should be in the stables," she explained.

Of course! The sisters needed their horses to travel. If the animals were not in the stables, the women would have left the chateau. He shifted his path toward the door to the inner ward. It was a good idea. He was impressed she had thought of it.

They emerged into a sunny ward. Tall stone walls rose high overhead. Beyond them, a thick band of dark clouds churned on the horizon. Guards strolled the walkways of the chateau gate. A bell rang out. A monk hurried through the ward toward the chapel, otherwise, the yard was empty.

Landyn stepped down the two stairs into the ward and led the way toward the back of the chateau and the stables. Tings could be heard coming from the blacksmith shop as they passed. The scent of fresh bread wafted through the air from the bakery. Soft prayers sounded from the chapel.

When they neared the wooden stables, a young boy of about eight summers rushed out to meet them. He brushed his scraggly brown hair from his eyes. "Ya need yer horse, Sir Landyn?" He hurried to match steps with Landyn.

"Not yet," Landyn answered. He cast a quick glance at the tumultuous clouds and hoped he would be on his way before the rain. He pushed the door of the stables open and entered.

The boy hesitated beside him, confused. "Is there something I can get ya?"

"You remember my sisters, don't you, Will?" Raven asked.

Landyn was surprised she knew the boy's name. He didn't even know it.

The boy nodded enthusiastically. "'Course. The ladies with swords."

Raven nodded. "Are their horses still here?"

Will frowned and swiped his hair from his eyes again. "'Course. And I'm takin' good care of 'em."

"The ladies didn't ride out of the castle?" Landyn queried.

"No. Their horses are there." He pointed down the row of stalls.

Raven walked down the aisle.

"I'm feeding 'em. Brushing 'em," Will explained with pride.

Raven paused at one stall, staring in bewilderment at the horse. She slightly shook her head.

"You haven't seen the ladies?" Landyn asked the boy.

Will shook his head. "I've been here all morn. They haven't come in."

Landyn glanced at Raven. She stood before the stall, tapping her finger against her thigh. Frustration welled inside him. While he sympathized about Raven's concern for her sisters, he was anxious to be back with John. Yet John had tasked him with finding the women. Where could her sisters be? "We'll check back with the monks," Landyn called to her.

Raven nodded slowly and returned to his side. "They couldn't have just disappeared."

No. They couldn't.

Raven glanced at the boy. "If you see them, tell them to wait for me."

Will nodded. "Aye."

Raven bowed her head and departed the stables.

Landyn followed. "We'll find them," he reassured. If they weren't in the chateau, perchance they had left the chateau on foot. "Where did you last see them?"

"Sage was with Brother Nicolas. Willow was following me. And then she wasn't."

"Perchance she saw something of interest or someone she knew," Landyn suggested, leading her back to the keep.

"Willow doesn't know anyone here," Raven stated and sighed. "It doesn't make sense."

Landyn agreed. It was strange no one had seen them.

A monk hurried toward them as they entered through the large doors of the keep. "The women are not in the chateau. We've checked everywhere," the thin monk insisted. "Everyone has been searching. Everywhere has been searched. No one has seen them."

Raven locked eyes with Landyn. It was the most distressed look he had ever seen.

His heart twisted but he turned to the monk. "Any sign of a struggle?"

"No," the monk replied. "No struggle. Nothing out of place. They must have left."

Raven shook her head. "Their horses are still here. And they would not have left the chateau without me."

"Keep searching," Landyn ordered the monk.

The monk's shoulders drooped. "Yes, sir."

Landyn watched him walk past them down the hallway. He knew the sisters were not here. The monks would have found them by now. Had they departed on foot? Run? Were they being chased? Still, someone should have seen them. Unless. He paused. Unless they had not escaped Brother Nicolas's murderer. Sage had been with the monk. Had she been harmed? Killed? If that were the case, where was her body? And what of the other sister? He hoped the sisters were alive, perhaps hiding somewhere in fear. But if Raven were any inclination of the natures of her sisters, they would never cower in fear.

As the monk moved away from them, Landyn saw three armored men cross the hallway at an intersection. One man wore black armor. Prickles raced along the nape of Landyn's neck. While it wasn't uncommon for knights to rest at the chateau, something about these three men set off alarms. He started to go after them.

"Perhaps they are not here," Raven whispered.

Landyn looked at her and then glanced toward the intersection. The men were gone. While his instincts told him they were a danger, he had another mission to accomplish. Raven. What was he going to do with her if they couldn't find her sisters? Where would she be safe? He had to get back to John. But he couldn't leave her at the chateau.

"Maybe they searched for me, couldn't find me, and left together for Sybil's farm. We're supposed to meet there if we get separated." She sighed and shook her head. "No. They would have taken their horses."

She knew as well as he did that something was not right. Everyone was suspect. No one was trustworthy. John and he agreed King Philip was after the Templar treasure. They were certain the chateau was being watched by spies for Philip. The chateau itself was not safe and, in fact, could have already been infiltrated by Philip's men. The Templars were trying to relocate the treasure safely and secretly. It was imperative that he help John.

Landyn considered his options. The sisters couldn't be found, but he couldn't abandon Raven at the chateau. The safest place for her was with him.

It was settled then. He knew what to do. "We will leave a missive for your sisters in case they are found. We will join your father."

Raven didn't like leaving the chateau. But she didn't know what else to do.

She and Landyn rode down the road, their horses kicking up clumps of mud as they galloped. She and Landyn had trotted their horses through a torrential downpour, passing farmers' fields and forests. The rain had slowed them, but they didn't stop.

Why would her sisters have left her? There was only one reason. They would have left — if they were forced to.

Landyn suddenly stopped, holding out his hand to halt.

Raven brought her horse to a standstill beside him. She looked around. They were approaching what appeared to be a woodland on one side of the road, tall trees stretching above their heads. On the other side of the road, a long grassy meadow blanketed the landscape. Only crickets' chirps and breaths from the horses could be heard. She waited.

His horse was as still as he was. The ends of his damp black hair curled at his shoulders. His gaze scanned the line of trees ahead. Finally, he relaxed and urged his horse on.

"What are you looking for?" Raven asked, spurring her horse to walk beside his.

He persisted in examining the surrounding

trees. "Robbers." He shrugged. "Anyone who might attack us."

She narrowed her eyes. She didn't believe that for an instant. He was looking for something or someone specific. "You needn't be frightened." She smiled sarcastically. "I'll protect you." She urged Thunder into a trot.

The rain had turned the road into mud, making it easy to see the lines from multiple carts and many horse hooves.

As the sun headed downward, Raven and Landyn proceeded down the road.

Ahead, the slosh of horse's hooves in the mud echoed through the trees.

They rounded a bend and mounted Templar Knights came into view. As they rode closer, Raven saw a squadron of knights riding beside three wagons, each wagon holding three wooden crates. She eyed the guarded wagons and the crates in them, surmising something of importance was inside.

A horse carrying her father charged up to them. He came to a halt, mud flying about her horse's legs. Worry and anger battled in his eyes. "What happened?"

"Your daughters were not at the chateau," Landyn explained.

Her father's stare snapped to her. "Raven?"

"Their horses were still stabled there," she replied sullenly.

He lifted his focus to the road behind them,

torn.

Raven waited for him to give the order to return to the chateau. She felt guilty that, as leader and the oldest sister, she couldn't find them. "I would have gone after them, but I didn't know where to start."

Landyn nodded. "It was as if they had disappeared."

"No one just disappears," her father answered, displeased. He steadied his horse and his lips thinned before he turned his gaze to Raven. "You should have followed my instructions and waited at Sybil's farm."

Raven took his harsh reprimand like a bolt to the heart. She nodded, bearing full responsibility for their disappearance.

The knights and wagons traveled by them.

"John," Landyn said quietly. "Brother Nicolas was murdered."

Her father straightened in the saddle, his fingers tightened around the reins, his expression filled with anxiety.

Raven stared at her father. He must return to the chateau now. He had to be as worried as she was about Sage and Willow.

His cheek rippled as he clenched his teeth. He scanned the wagons and then the horizon. "It's almost nightfall," her father said and looked at Landyn. "We're not going to make it to Robert's farm. The rain and muddy road slowed us down."

Raven glanced at the surrounding landscape. Thick trees of a forest spread out on one side of the road and an open hill on the other. The trees would offer them protection from the elements, but they could also hide robbers.

"Send scouts," her father told Landyn. "Inform Robert we will not be stopping. Send some knights into the forest to search. I don't want to be ambushed here."

Landyn nodded and spurred his horse toward the troops, shouting orders.

Raven watched him for a moment. Her father was happy with Landyn. No, his anger was directed solely at her. She urged her steed beside her father's. "You're not going back to the chateau?"

"For what reason? You said the girls were not there."

She shook her head in confusion. "What about Sage and Willow?"

He turned a harsh stare on her. "We will meet them at Sybil's. That was our plan if we got separated." He stiffened his jaw. "You girls should be there now."

Another reprimand. Downtrodden, she sat atop her weary steed, soaked to the bone. The storm had drenched her. The water ran beneath her leather armor onto her chemise. She felt like a sodden rat.

Her father cast a disparaging look at her before galloping toward the front of the caravan.

Raven's fingers curled around the reins. She was worried about Sage and Willow, but there was nothing she could do now. She urged her horse after her father, calling, "Father."

He paused.

She halted her horse at his side, lifting her chin. "I can help you," she insisted. "I am as skilled as any of these knights. You know I am."

His hair was tied back away from his face. A dark beard was beginning to shadow his chin. "I told you and your sisters to wait at Sybil's farm," her father countered. "You were not supposed to be here. It is dangerous. I didn't want to involve you girls in this."

Raven and her sisters had worked with their father many times before, but on jobs he believed were safe. This one was different. There was a reason he had not asked them to accompany him. A risky one. "But I'm here now. Shouldn't I know what to expect?"

His lips tightened. He shook his head and straightened in the saddle. "Stay near me. And this time, follow instructions."

His disapproval made her feel as if someone were stepping on her chest. It felt tight. She hadn't meant to disappoint him. Her shoulders drooped and she nodded.

Her father trotted his steed to the front of the line of men.

Raven skimmed the caravan again. The knights wore the white tunic emblazoned with a red cross. Some dismounted their steeds and led them to the forest to tie their reins to the trees. Other knights urged their horses closer to the wagons to guard them.

Her eyes focused on the wagons. What was in those crates? Something worthy of guarding, something precious or expensive.

Contents her father didn't want her to know about.

Thunder nickered and tossed his head.

She rubbed his neck. "Don't you start," she whispered and rode him to her father's side.

He swung his leg over his horse and

dismounted.

Raven glanced again at the trees. As the sun set, it cast a red glow across the leaves. She didn't like stopping here. Unease filled her and yet, she couldn't explain why. She shivered slightly.

"Are you well?" her father asked.

She jerked her attention to him. Damp strands of his dark hair hung around his face and yet he still maintained his strength of character and his commanding presence. It was why there were legends about him. Why everyone knew his name. She nodded.

"I shall have a fire lit," he said. "You can warm yourself there."

"No, Father," Raven objected. "It's not safe."

"You are chilled. Landyn!" He strode toward Landyn, ignoring her protests.

Raven swung her leg over Thunder and dismounted. She reached out to stop him.

"Have a small fire started so Raven can warm herself," he ordered as Landyn neared.

Landyn's gaze swiveled to her and then he nodded.

Raven groaned inwardly and ground her teeth. Yes, the delicate woman needs a fire started. How humiliating! Now, Landyn must think she was as weak as a pampered lady. She would have been fine with a blanket, just like the rest of the knights.

Landyn rode off to convey the order.

"I don't need a fire, Father," she protested. "I have a blanket in my bag."

He stared hard at her.

In the dying sunlight, Raven saw that look. The look of tenderness for his one flaw. His love for his daughters. She was certain he was as concerned for Sage and Willow as she was and that he had a good reason for not going to find them. She shook her head slightly. "It's dangerous," she protested weakly.

"Not as dangerous as you becoming ill."

After losing her mother to illness, such things were always on his mind. She relented with a nod. She would keep the fire small and try to shelter the light from the outside world. The other knights would probably gather round it, too. They must be as chilled as she was. If her father thought it was safe, then she would comply.

Still, she glanced warily at the trees and bushes along the side of the road. This was not a place she would pick to rest. Unease snaked up her spine.

As he moved toward the crates, she followed him, asking, "Who is coming after you?"

He scowled in confusion.

She straightened. "These knights are guarding those crates. You've sent scouts ahead and into the forest. Who are you searching for?"

His lips thinned. "You are safe. You need not worry." He turned to continue toward the wagons.

She stepped into his path. "I'm not a child. I can help if I know what to look for."

He stared at her for a long, contemplative moment. His eyes softened, and he grinned. "I know you are capable." His grin vanished. "But you disobey me. I gave you orders to go to Sybil's farm."

Guilt and disappointment filled her soul. He was right, but she could not have let Sage go to Chateau le Bezu alone.

He moved around her.

Raven watched him go. She couldn't escape the regret she felt. She was the one in charge and she was supposed to look out for her sisters, even though Sage had not listened to her. Raven bowed her head. And now, her sisters were missing. She would find them. But currently, she had to listen to her father's instructions. She had to prove to him that she was capable, that she was a dutiful daughter.

She strolled back to her horse. She had to earn his respect.

Landyn was tense and jumpy. He had to calm down. He rolled his shoulders atop his horse as he glanced at the trees on the side of the road. Scouts had been sent into the forest to make sure there were no men lurking there. Even if there were not any men in this forest, he knew an attack was coming. Eventually, they would be ambushed for the treasure those crates supposedly contained. King Philip wanted it too badly.

Only a select few of the Templar Knights knew what the plan was, what was actually in those crates. But this mission was important, and the knights had willingly come. As had John.

Landyn had known John for a long time, and he admired him. It was John who had first come up with this clever plan. They were heading to Peniscola Port in an attempt to draw the king's men away from the real treasure. But neither he nor John believed they would make it that far before they were ambushed. They both thought the Templar

Knights would be able to fight off a force of the king's men. He scanned the line of Templar Knights. Even if they expected to be victorious, some of these men could die.

That was why John didn't want Raven with them.

He glanced at Raven. She was beside her father; both were checking their horses' hooves. She was a mirror of him in many ways, but also tinier, curvier. Her leather armor could not hide her rounded breasts and shapely hips. When Raven and John finished, they both led their horses to the trees. John wrapped the reins about a tree branch while Raven draped hers over.

Landyn's gaze rested on Raven again. She took the offered flask from her father and drank. Her black hair hung in a braid down her back to her bottom. He mentally scoffed. Such a long braid would impede fighting; he would have cut it long ago. She was but a slip of a woman and he had been surprised that John had sired such a thin girl. He had always pictured John's daughters being stout and more...muscular.

Raven looked directly at Landyn then. Her blue eyes sparkled in the setting sun. He hadn't noticed that her eye color was blue. Not that it mattered. Only that his wife, Viola, had blue eyes. But she was nothing like John's daughter.

He glanced over his shoulder at the knights and the wagons. A third of the men strolled the perimeter on guard duty while the others settled in for the night, sitting on the ground, leaning against the wagons. They would switch off at allotted times.

John strode down the road past him. He

stopped near a wagon and bent to inspect the wheels. Landyn snuck another glance at Raven.

She checked the buckle on the horse's bridle and ran a hand beneath it between the leather and the horse.

She and John were so similar, Landyn thought with amusement. He dismounted and grasped the reins, leading the steed to John and Raven's horses. He tossed the reins over a tree branch and ran a hand over the black steed's neck. "I'm sorry we didn't find your sisters."

Raven nodded.

"This must be difficult for you."

She shrugged. "Father and I will meet up with them. They must be at Sybil's farm." She put a hand on her hip and jerked her chin at the wagons. "The contents of those crates must be important."

Landyn grunted softly and turned away from her to his horse. He bent to inspect the saddle straps.

"Treasure," she whispered.

He hesitated in his inspection for a moment before straightening and moving to the steed's leather bridle. "What do you mean?"

"The only thing worthy of so much protection is gold. Priceless relics. Treasure."

He shifted to her, keeping his face emotionless.

She shrugged again. "If it were me, I would have disguised it better."

He examined her. She was confident and overly perceptive. But he should have known this. She was trained by John.

She grinned and stepped past him.

He watched her walk to John. The slight sway of her hips, the curves of her feminine form beneath her leather armor apparent to all who would look. She was nothing like Viola.

CHAPTER FOUR

The moon shone down in the cloudless sky, illuminating the landscape in a muted white glow. Long shadows fell over the road from the trees. The croaks of frogs and chirps of crickets sounded through the darkness.

Raven's clothing was almost completely dry. The small bonfire before her was nearly extinguished. She watched the dying embers for a moment before scanning the surrounding area. Three knights stretched out across from her, sleeping. The one in the center emitted a rumbling snore, rivaling the frogs.

Her father sat beside her, running an oiled cloth over his sword. She had always tried to be the daughter he wanted her to be. She had always sought to make him proud. At the thought of her failure, her gaze dashed away from him and over to Landyn. He rested on the opposite side of her father, his arms crossed over his chest, his knees bent as if ready to spring into action. His eyes were closed, as if he were asleep. Why was her father so confident in his ability? Where had he met Landyn? Why did her father trust him and confide in him?

She bowed her head. She shouldn't be here. She should be with Sage and Willow at Sybil's farm. Not on the road with a bunch of Templar Knights and crickets.

The gurgling snore sounded through the night air.

Raven sat up straight. The noise from the crickets and frogs had ceased. Her gaze swung to the shadowed trees. She eased herself to her feet and reached for her weapon. "Father," she warned.

He looked at her and stood immediately, sliding his sword from its sheath. "On your feet!" he commanded.

Landyn jumped up instantly, pulling his weapon free of its sheath.

They stood still, expecting, listening. Tense.

Raven glared into the shadows beneath the trees. The attack would come from that way. They could not hide anywhere else. Someone was out there.

Everything froze. Her father was like a statue, unmoving and waiting. Landyn took a step up to his side, his sword reflected in the moonlight.

Time stretched. No one attacked. No one came for them. The knights eased their stances, relaxing.

Raven knew someone was out there. The crickets remained silent. The air was quiet.

Her father finally inhaled a deep breath. "It must be an animal," he announced.

Raven knew it was no animal that had silenced nature.

"Raven," her father commanded. "Go and scout behind us."

She looked at him in surprise. "*Behind* us?"

"Yes," he replied. "To make sure no one is there. Landyn, go with her."

Landyn glanced at him in astonishment, but finally nodded, sheathing his sword.

Raven was reluctant to put her weapon away. She took two steps toward her horse, her gaze fixed on the shadows among the trees. Why send her to scout behind them? On their ride toward the squad, she and Landyn had not encountered anyone. She sheathed her weapon and quickly mounted Thunder.

When Landyn was atop his steed, they galloped down the road.

As they passed the wagons, Raven gazed curiously at the crates, wondering what was in them.

Landyn resisted the urge to look over his shoulder toward the caravan as he rode after Raven down the road. Why was John sending his daughter away? Was someone in the forest? And if there was, why hadn't he sent another knight to guard his daughter? Landyn's skills would have been better used fighting.

As they rounded the bend in the road, Raven drew up short, scanning the area. "Why would Father send us backward?"

"He's trying to protect you," Landyn said firmly.

"From what?" she demanded. "Perhaps if I understood what was happening, who we were scouting for, I would be more helpful."

"You weren't supposed to be here."

Her stare pinned him like a red-hot poker. "But I am."

Landyn nodded. She was right. There was no use arguing the point.

They searched the area, ambling down the muddy road. This was a waste of time. There was no one in the forest. It was too early for an attack. He and John expected a battle closer to the Peniscola Port. For an attack to come this quickly in the journey, the king's men would have had to be near the chateau when the caravan departed.

"If you haven't found anything, we should return." Landyn waited for her to turn her horse toward the caravan.

She didn't move for a long moment, shifting her gaze back to the chateau. Her back was straight, her hands firm around the reins. She was comfortable on the horse, sitting like a man. He had heard about John's daughters from the monks. Some thought them an abomination because of their manlike talents and dress. Others found them fascinating. Both groups had grudging admiration for their skills.

Landyn thought Raven was interesting. "Your father is waiting," he added.

She sighed softly through clenched teeth, and it almost came out as a hiss. Then, suddenly, she frowned. She urged her horse away from the caravan.

He glanced anxiously back toward the caravan.

It was not visible down the road, and he didn't like leaving it. But John had tasked him with making sure Raven was unharmed. So, he followed her.

She stopped at the side of the road, staring at the ground.

Landyn followed her gaze. The moonlight washed over part of the road that many hoofprints had smashed. His eyes tracked the trail along the road where the caravan was resting. "It's our men."

She urged her horse to the side so Landyn could see the wet weeds on the side of the road. Another large group of tracks trailed off the road into the trees. "Then why do they lead into the forest?"

Panic grasped Landyn in a cold fist, and he whirled his horse, spurring him into a charge down the road.

He had to warn them!

Raven bent low over the saddle, urging Thunder faster as she dashed after Landyn. What had happened to the scouts in the forest? How could no one have seen that many men?

Before they came within visual distance of the caravan, the tings of metal against metal and the cries of men rang through the air.

Dread clawed at Raven.

Landyn stopped ahead of her.

She was going to race by him, but he moved his horse into her path. "Wait," he ordered.

She clenched her teeth, and her fingers gripped the reins so tightly that Thunder reared up onto two legs. When the horse landed his front hooves in the mud, she quickly scanned the road ahead.

The ground was strewn with white-tunicked Templar Knights, as well as other knights in black.

Raven scowled. Black knights. That was why she hadn't seen anyone in the forest. Farther up the road, the remaining Templar Knights had formed a circle around the wagons. A large group of black-clad knights approached slowly, holding their swords before them. The Templar Knights were massively outnumbered. Even if she and Landyn joined them, they would still be overwhelmed.

"This way," he said and headed into the forest.

Raven hesitated. Where was her father? She quickly scanned the Templar Knights and their opponents, but she couldn't see him. With a grimace of uncertainty, she spurred Thunder and followed Landyn into the forest. Just past the tree line, he dismounted.

She quickly followed his lead, swinging her leg over the saddle and landing on the ground. They moved swiftly from tree to tree to stay hidden.

Raven ducked beneath branches and stepped over fallen branches. She looked toward the road. Through breaks in the shadowed tree line, flashes of white tunics shone in the moonlight as the knights fought.

She crouched slightly and glanced at the ground. The muddy floor of leaves was trampled by footsteps. An ambush. She had been right about someone being in the forest, but she couldn't have imagined the number of men. She peered back toward the wagons. Clangs resonated through the night air as the battle continued. She caught glimpses of the black knights. They wore no heraldry. Who were they?

And where was her father?

Landyn stopped and bent behind a bush, peering through the leaves.

Raven sheltered beside him, following his stare. She angled her head so she could see through the branches. The wagons were before them with only a few Templar Knights left. One rushed toward a black knight, holding his sword before him. They crossed blades. The Templar Knight swung his mighty weapon around to the side. The black knight blocked the blow.

Another black knight came up behind the Templar Knight and shoved his blade into his back.

Raven inhaled in surprised disgust.

Landyn nudged Raven with his elbow and stood, moving to another tree. Laughter echoed from somewhere on the road. A scream of agony pierced the air.

Raven trailed Landyn, keeping low. There were so many black knights. The Templar Knights had no chance of defeating them. She heard guffaws coming from the road and paused to glance back.

A gentle breeze shifted the tree branches and leaves, allowing her to see a Templar Knight on his knees in the middle of the road. A group of black-tunicked knights surrounded him. One kicked him to the ground. Another hit him with the flat edge of his sword.

He needed help. Raven rose to help him.

Landyn grabbed her arm and pulled her to another tall bush beside a tree. "Your father," he whispered.

She glanced at Landyn. He was staring intently

in another direction down the road with a frown on his brow.

She followed his stare and her stomach rolled in dread.

Her father was captured between two black clothed knights, his jaw tight with hate.

"Father," she whispered and jerked forward, but Landyn pulled her back.

"There's too many men," Landyn whispered.

Raven clenched her fists. She had to get to her father and help him, but she knew Landyn was right. Still, the need to aid her father swirled inside of her like a raging tornado.

A tall man with scraggly blond hair clasped a sword in one hand. With the other, he reached out and ripped something from her father's neck. He held it up with a smile before wrapping it around his neck and tying the cord.

Raven couldn't see what it was, but it was obviously a necklace of some sort. She tilted her head, straining for a better look.

The man with the blond hair turned away from her father.

Raven saw an eye patch covering one of his eyes. She clenched her teeth as tension stiffened her muscles. She mentally pleaded with the eye-patched man to let her father go.

Her father scowled fiercely. Never show any fear, he had told her.

But she was fearful. She was fearful of what would happen to him.

Then, the eye-patched man whirled and plunged his sword into her father's stomach.

Raven inhaled, her world tilting around her.

"Father," she gasped. She jerked forward to go to him, desolation cresting over her. But she couldn't move forward.

The eye-patched man slowly withdrew his bloody sword from her father's stomach.

The black guards released her father, and he crumpled to one knee, clutching his abdomen.

Raven trembled with disbelief and dread.

The blond-haired man sheathed his weapon. He circled her father before grabbing his chin and forcing him to look up at him. He spoke to her father.

From her position behind the trees, Raven couldn't hear the words but saw the twisting grimace of her father's response. Her gaze dropped to the hand wrapped around his stomach. In the darkness, she saw black liquid, her father's blood, dripping through his fingers. Panic gripped her in an icy fist. She lurched to go to him. Again, she couldn't move. Desperately, she looked down at her arm.

Landyn had a firm grip on her wrist, preventing her from moving. "It won't do either of you any good if you are both killed," he whispered.

She knew his words were true, but every instinct demanded she fight to defend her father.

Landyn's grip tightened over her forearm.

Raven logically knew there were too many of the black-tunicked men for them to fight and live. She couldn't win if she fought. All the Templar Knights had been overpowered. There were just too many opponents.

But it was her father. She trembled in despair. Her father had taught her to think and reason, to always remain in control of a situation. Her mind told her Landyn was correct. But every impulse she had demanded she fight for her father. Save him.

Finally, the blond-haired man shoved her father away, sending him into the mud of the road. He whirled, a dark cape flapping out behind him, and called to his men as he marched away.

Raven's gaze flitted from the man back to her father where he lay prone on the ground. Her heart hammered in her chest. She had to reach him.

Landyn's hand clenched her arm. "Wait," he warned.

The blond-haired man marched toward the wagons. The other men followed him.

Unable to wait another moment, she shook her arm free and immediately moved to a tree before the road. She glanced down the road in the direction of the wagons.

The black-tunicked men were mounting horses. The man with the blond hair was already atop his steed, charging away down the road toward le Bezu.

The crates on the wagons had all been opened. Two chests had been shoved from the first wagon and rested in the mud of the road with the inside of the wooden boxes visible. Two on the second wagon had been pushed onto their sides, one hanging precariously on the edge. All of them were empty.

Templar Knights in white tunics lay scattered over the road and around the wagon like pristine piles of flowers.

Raven looked back at her father. His knee was pointed up toward the sky, but he was still lying flat on his back. Not moving. She looked again at the retreating men as they galloped away.

"Raven," Landyn whispered.

Raven wasn't listening. She dashed across to the road and fell to her knees at her father's side. His eyes were closed. Her anguished stare swept his torso. His bloodied hand covered his abdomen. "Father." Her voice was a whisper ripped from her soul.

He winced and gritted his teeth, opening his eyes to slits.

Raven gasped hopefully.

He tried to sit up; his hand pressed tightly over his stomach. "You have to get out of here," he commanded.

She shook her head, refusing to leave. Blood oozed through his fingers. She had seen many wounds in her life. The location of his injury and the amount of blood he was losing were concerning. Her hands trembled as she reached for his injury.

"Landyn," he growled. "Get her out of here."

Landyn had come up behind her and took hold of her arm.

She tore her arm free of his hold. "I'm not leaving without you."

"I'll be well," her father said through clenched teeth.

She knew it was a lie. Blood pooled in the mud at his side, creating little swirls of red liquid in the rainwater. "Let me look at it."

He grabbed her hand, squeezing it. Blood smeared across her fingers and for a moment she could only stare at her father's blood on her skin.

"Raven," he growled.

She looked into his dark eyes. His face was ghastly pale. She knew death was coming.

"You have to leave," he commanded.

She shook her head.

"They'll come back. And I'm counting on you."

Her mind refused to focus. What was he talking about? She had to save his life.

"Raven, you have to find your sisters," he said. "You have to leave me."

Angered by his suggestion of abandoning him, she leaned toward him. For the second time in her life, she refused his direct command. Her voice wavered as she declared, "Hawkes don't leave Hawkes. You taught us that."

He stared into her eyes and with a sigh, he reclined back.

At that moment, she knew she would lose him. He would never relinquish command. And she would never admit defeat. She twisted toward the road and put her fingers to her lips to whistle loudly for Thunder.

Her father began to sit up with a frown on his face.

"Raven." Landyn protested her loud call.

She ignored him and gently pushed her father back. She began to unlace his leather armor. It wouldn't be the first time she had stitched up one of his wounds. She peeled aside the brown leather and was horrified by the amount of blood soaking his white tunic. She quickly removed his hand from the wound and lifted his bloodied tunic. The wound was on his abdomen, and it was deep. Red liquid squirted from the puncture, while even more flowed over his side like a river.

Tears filled her eyes. She would not admit to herself that it was a death blow, even though she knew the truth.

"Landyn," her father called.

Landyn fell to a knee at her father's side as she pressed down on the wound to stem the flow of blood.

Her father reached up and grasped Landyn's tunic in a clenched fist. "He has the key. It is for my daughters. Get it back."

Raven scowled in confusion and glanced at Landyn.

Landyn nodded and promised, "I will."

"Make sure they get it."

"I will."

Her father lay back with a sigh and released his hold on Landyn's tunic. "Take care of her," he told Landyn.

"Don't do that," she commanded him. "Don't you give up."

He grinned gently at her. "Never."

Hoofbeats sounded behind her. She looked over her shoulder as Thunder came to a halt behind her. She turned to stand, but her father caught her hand.

"You are the leader now, Raven," he said.

She refused to hear this. He was her father. He was the head of their family! She shook her head. "No, Father. It's not that bad. I can—"

He lifted his head closer to her. "Take care of your sisters."

"No," she whispered. "I'll wrap your wound and Landyn and I will get you to the chateau. You'll be…" Her voice choked. "Fine."

"Always remember that you are a Hawke." He stared into her eyes for a long moment before lying back.

She shook her head and placed a shaking hand over his wound. She continued to shake her head in denial. A sob wracked her body. As she pressed down on his stomach, she realized she could no longer feel his intake of breath.

This can't be happening, she told herself as she pushed harder.

"Raven," Landyn called softly.

"Get cloth from the saddlebag," she said in a thick voice.

"He's gone," Landyn said firmly.

Gone. The word sent tremors of disbelief and remorse through her. Her world slowed. She sniffled. He couldn't be gone. He was John Hawke. He could defeat anyone in battle. He could…

"Raven," Landyn uttered gently. He put his hand on her shoulder.

She barely felt his touch as her father's last words rang through her mind. She was in charge now. But she couldn't be. She didn't know half of what her father knew. She needed him. Tears blurred her vision of his strong, wounded body. She removed her hands from his wound and sat back on her heels. Her hands, covered in blood, lay limply against her black leggings. What was she to do?

How could she save her sisters? She couldn't even save her father. How could she save anyone if she couldn't help the one person that meant more than anything to her?

She swallowed heavily in a dry, thick throat.

"We should leave. They might be back," Landyn said.

"We have to bury him," Raven said without emotion, and sniffled again. She looked at her hands. They were covered in red.

"We have no tools. We can't do that here."

"Then we will bring him back to le Bezu," Raven said. Even though her body was numb, her lips and her mind still worked. But she couldn't stand. She couldn't move.

Her father was dead.

CHAPTER FIVE

Landyn searched the felled Templar Knights and took what he could carry to return to le Bezu. He retrieved his horse and, on the way back to Raven, gathered the reins of any horses that remained.

She knelt at her father's side, and sympathy washed over him. He reached out a hand to her, but then lowered it. While John was a good friend of his and Landyn would miss him, he was Raven's father. Nothing could comfort that loss. Nothing he said would wipe away her grief. He remembered when his own father passed. He had been just a boy, and still he recalled how shocked and distraught he had been seeing his father lowered into the earth.

He dropped the reins of the horses and led John's steed forward. He looked at Raven's slouched shoulders. Her bloodied hands were curled before her in her lap and her gaze was on the ground.

Landyn tugged open a string on one of his steed's saddlebags. He removed a cloth and returned to her side. Bending to one knee, he reached for her hand.

She lifted her gaze to him.

He was struck by the complete devastation in her eyes. Tears ringed her thick lashes, but as far as he could tell, she had not shed one drop.

He collected one of her hands. As he wiped the blood from her hand, he noticed how small it was compared to his. He carefully and gently scrubbed her palm until her tan skin emerged from the deep red. Then he eased her hand down. Before he could grasp her other one, she slid the cloth from his fingers and began to work on it. Her fingers rubbed her thumb with the cloth and pushed the material over her palm.

He shifted his gaze to her face. Her skin was flawless, her cheekbones high. There was a slight scowl on her brow and her almond-shaped eyes were heavy with sadness. "He was a good man," Landyn told her. It was a weak statement of sentiment, but he couldn't convey his loss.

She paused her movements before continuing to wipe her hand without acknowledging him.

"Will you be well?" he asked.

Again, she hesitated, clenching the cloth in a fisted grip. Her chin quivered before she murmured, "Of course." She swallowed, lifted her chin, and stood. She straightened her back. "Let's get my father on his horse and head back to le Bezu."

Landyn looked down the road. "The men who attacked us headed that way. We'll have to be careful."

Her lip curled in a sneer and hatred burned in her eyes. "Who were they?"

"I believe they were the king's men. But I can't

prove it."

"And the man with the eye patch. Who is he?"

Landyn faltered. "Why do you ask?"

"He is a walking dead man," she explained coldly.

Landyn bridled. Her hatred was all-consuming. It poured out from her heart, threatening to scorch all in its path. He recognized this darkness. She was going after the man with the eye patch. She was going to kill him. He shook his head, denying her the information. "John wouldn't have wanted this path for you. He said to find your sisters."

Raven nodded, standing. "And that is exactly what I plan to do. After I find my father's murderer." She tossed the cloth aside and stepped up to her horse.

Landyn gazed at her in shock. He was familiar with intense anger and remorse, her need for vengeance, from personal experience. But it didn't help. It couldn't help her heal. "Killing him will not bring your father back."

"No," she agreed with a clenched jaw. "But it will send a message to everyone else — never hurt my family."

He grabbed her arm. "Find your sisters. Don't let the rage consume you."

She pulled her arm free. "I'm not asking for your approval." Raven took the reins of John's horse and guided it into position beside her father.

Landyn stood firmly rooted in discontentment. She was on a deadly, lonely path. And if John hadn't asked him to take care of her, he would have left her. He didn't want to be swept into that darkness again. It had taken him a long time to break free of it.

She bent down and grabbed her father beneath his shoulders.

He clenched his lips. John's final order was to look out for her. He owed his friend at least that much. Landyn stalked to Raven's side and indicated John's feet with a tip of his chin.

Raven relinquished her father's shoulders and moved to his feet.

Together, they lifted him and placed him over his horse. Landyn pushed him up, situating him so he wouldn't fall.

Raven mounted her horse.

Landyn gathered up the reins of the other horses and tied them to his steed's saddle. Then he mounted his own.

Raven took the lead, moving slowly past the wagons. Her gaze swiveled to look at the open crates.

Landyn cringed. He knew she would be angry when she found out why they were empty. He sighed softly. She was going to be a lot of trouble for him. He had planned to help her find her sisters and leave her to their care. But he hadn't imagined her need for revenge. If John had not asked him to care for her, Landyn would see her back to le Bezu and depart. She was on a path that could lead only to death.

The horses needed to rest and so they paused as the sun began to rise over the horizon.

Raven wanted to keep going. She wanted to reach the chateau as soon as possible. She was restless and on edge. Her muscles clenched as she stood beneath a tree, near a stream where Thunder and the other horses drank. Her gaze was on the road, and she crossed her arms, swaying from side to side as if ready to run. The only thing she could see in her mind was the man with the eye patch. Her upper lip curled, and her body shook. He had brutally killed her father.

"Raven," Landyn called.

She swiveled her gaze to him. Landyn held out a flask. She shook her head and turned her stare back to the road. She would find that man with the eye patch and kill him for what he'd done.

She glanced at her father's body hanging over his horse. Grief welled inside her. She still couldn't believe he was dead. It didn't seem real. She didn't even know why he had died, what his last mission really was. Those crates. Had the men taken what was inside of them? Or had they been empty to begin with?

All those Templar Knights had fought to defend what was inside of the crates and lost their lives doing so. She shook her head. Even if it had been treasure, it was a waste of good lives.

Chills raced along her shoulders. Empty crates? Her sisters missing? An unexplained job that sent her father to his death? Brother Nicolas's murder? It was all too much to handle.

She took a breath and refocused. Nothing mattered except for finding the man with the eye patch.

"What are your sisters' names?" Landyn asked, coming up beside her. "Willow and…"

"Sage," Raven answered. Of course, he would

know of Willow. Every man had at least heard of her. She was beautiful and appealing to men. Raven didn't know if it was Willow's beautiful blonde hair, her charisma, or both. But men found her irresistible.

Sage was quiet and smart. Brilliantly smart. She could pick locks without trouble. She could figure out any puzzle quicker than any of them.

Raven loved both her sisters. She didn't know how she was going to tell them their father was dead. And that she was with him but couldn't save him. It was her job to protect the family. As the oldest, she was supposed to look out for her sisters, and she didn't even know where they were. It would have been easy to blame Sage for insisting they go to the chateau instead of following her father's orders. But Raven knew she was just as responsible as either of her sisters. If only she had tried harder to talk Sage out of translating the book, they would be together. Sadness fell upon her like a black cloud. She swallowed past a lump in her throat and bowed her head. She had failed her family.

"You couldn't have saved him," Landyn said.

Shocked, she turned to him. She shook her head. "You are wrong."

His eyes glided over her face. They were dark like his hair. His jaw was square and strong. "If you had tried, you would have been dead alongside him. There were too many men."

She peered down at the brown earth beneath her booted feet. "At least I wouldn't have failed trying to defend him."

"What about your sisters? Who would tell them what happened? Who would look out for them?"

She clenched her teeth. He was using her father's order against her. She nodded. "I will look out for them. I will. After I find the man with the eye patch."

"This is a dangerous path you are seeking," Landyn advised.

"I won't let my father's murder go unpunished," she vowed and stole another glance at her father's body draped over the horse.

Landyn shook his head in disapproval. "You don't know what you're getting into."

"Then tell me. Tell me why you are keeping the identity of the man with the eye patch a secret. Tell me why those crates were empty. Tell me what was worth my father's life."

Landyn took a deep breath. "It won't help you."

"It will make it easier for me. I'm going to find out with or without your help." She pushed herself away from the tree and approached him. "If my father was your friend as you proclaim, you would want the same thing I do."

Landyn bowed his head, his black hair falling forward to cover his face. "Your father's killer will get what's due to him. But it doesn't have to be by your hand." He swiveled his gaze to her. "Trust me, Raven. I've been where you are. Your anger can become uncontrollable. This will consume you."

"You watched your father be murdered?" she asked in a mocking tone. "You haven't been where I am. I am a Hawke, and we look out for our family." She lifted her chin. Even as she proclaimed this, her heart ached for her father.

"Not all of your family is gone," he reminded her quietly.

Her mind wavered between her need for vengeance and the thought of her missing sisters. "You're right. And when I tell them how our father was murdered, they will want vindication also."

"Raven..." Landyn pleaded.

She didn't want to hear him. "What I don't understand is—what was in those crates? If they held treasure, as I suspected, where was the treasure?"

Landyn looked away to the horses.

"What are you hiding?" she mused. "You knew about that job. You knew what was in those crates."

Landyn bowed his head, refusing to relinquish the secrets.

She stepped back. "Then I have no choice but to find the man with the eye patch. He'll have answers."

They rode to the top of the hill where the beige stones of the Chateau le Bezu's walls stood tall against the blue morning sky like a painting. Its four turrets boxed the fortress. The sun shone down over the surrounding grassy lands of gently rolling hills.

Landyn was exhausted from riding the entire night. They had only stopped once. His gaze again settled on Raven. Her back was straight in determination. Wasn't she tired? How did she do it? He knew that at times, rage and sorrow left one unable to sleep. He recognized the anger in her clenched fists as they gripped the reins. If it were raining, he was certain steam would have risen from her skin.

He was keeping secrets from her, secrets he believed would add fire to her fury. The crates. The name of the man with the eye patch. He knew it was only time before she discovered the answers. He should just tell her and let her go on her own destructive path.

Landyn shook his head and groaned silently to himself. John had asked him to look after her. If it weren't for this final request from his friend, Landyn would have gladly allowed her ride off alone. He knew revenge was a lethal path. And that was why he had to stay with her. To help her. He owed John that. John had saved him.

Once they found her sisters and her need for revenge abated, he would continue his training to become a Templar.

His loyalty as an upcoming Templar Knight was to the order. He had planned to take the Holy Order vows within the month and become a full Templar Knight. But now, his focus was on Raven. He was hoping to find Raven's sisters and set her on a better path.

He rode behind her, past the outer walls of the chateau and into the inner ward. He dismounted and when Will rushed out to greet him, he gave him orders to see to all the horses and to tell Father Michel they needed a burial.

The boy cast a glance at John's body and nodded.

As Raven walked toward the double wooden doors of the chateau, Landyn asked him, "Have you seen the two women?"

"No, sir," Will answered, scratching his head. "Their horses are still stabled, but they are missing."

Landyn patted the boy's brown head and trailed Raven. He knew her heart was broken, and he had hoped her sisters could talk sense into her. He would escort her to Sybil's farm and return to the chateau.

"Sir!" the boy called.

Landyn paused and turned to him.

"The commander wishes to speak to you," the boy added.

Landyn glanced back at the chateau. The commander? Yes, he should report to the commander. He and John had spoken to him before they departed about the importance of the mission. But no one expected an attack this early into the trip. They had planned to make it at least halfway to Peniscola before fighting. And he had never expected Boucher, the man with the eye patch, to be leading the attack.

Pierre Boucher. Landyn tried to relax, but his shoulder muscles tensed. He had hoped never to see him again. His jaw clenched. Everything returned as if it had happened yesterday. Her scream. The blood.

Landyn quickly pushed the memories aside and hurried to catch up with Raven. "Where are you going?"

"To get food and supplies," she responded.

Landyn mentally groaned. She was determined. He stepped before her to halt her. "We should go to Sybil's farm."

Her eyebrows rose in surprise. "We?" She smiled mockingly. "I will go there after I find the man that killed my father."

"How will you do that?"

"I'll start by talking to some of the monks and knights. Find out who that man with the eye patch is."

"You should wait until your father is buried," Landyn advised.

Her flashing blue eyes narrowed. "Why? My father is gone. And the longer I wait, the farther away his murderer gets."

Landyn nodded. "At the very least, you should eat." He flagged down a passing knight. "Please see Raven to the kitchens."

"What are you going to do?" she asked suspiciously.

"I have responsibilities," he said.

Her eyes slitted as if she didn't believe him, but she nodded. "I thank you for your help with my father. I'm certain you were a good friend to him."

As she turned away, confusion settled around him. It sounded as if she was saying goodbye, but his mission was not over. "Raven," he called. When she paused and spun to him, he continued, "I will see you after John's burial."

She concurred and followed the monk.

He watched her walk away, the gentle shift of her hips, her curvy bottom and wondered if she knew her bottom swayed with each step. He mentally shook himself. She was an unforeseen problem. He had not expected John to task him with her safety. Still, there were things he needed to do here. Then, he would find her and…

And what? What was he to do with her? She was stubborn, determined, and bent on a path of destruction. And yet, she was vulnerable. She was unlike any woman he had encountered before.

The problem was, part of him understood her need for revenge. Although it had taken him a long time to heal, there was a part of him that still wanted that revenge.

There was only one place to go. One thing to do to cleanse himself of these feelings.

CHAPTER SIX

Raven waited until the knight leading her to the kitchens rounded a corner. Then, she excused herself by professing exhaustion. She turned quickly back down the hallway to follow Landyn. He knew more than he was telling her. He'd said he had responsibilities. What responsibilities did he have? He should be concerned with the group of black-tunicked men who had killed the Templar Knights. And finding the man with the eye patch.

She trailed Landyn stealthily, being careful to remain out of his eyesight. He was hard not to notice. He was taller than the monks and most of the knights. His thick, wavy hair hung to his broad shoulders. His gait was confident and powerful.

He entered a room through the open doors.

Raven paused at the opening, pressing herself against the stone wall. She twisted her neck and peeked in.

A table covered with a plain white cloth was at the front of the room with a wooden cross in the center. Behind this, a large cross hung on the wall. Chairs lined the room, facing the table. It was a chapel.

Raven's eyebrows rose in surprise. What kind of responsibilities could Landyn have here? Did he need to speak with the priest?

Landyn's boots echoed as he walked up the aisle.

There was one other man kneeling in the front row. Was that who Landyn was meeting?

He dropped to a knee before the altar and made the sign of the cross, touching his forehead, chest, and each shoulder. Then he knelt on the stone floor and clasped his hands.

Raven stared in confusion. He was praying! She never would have marked him as a religious man. But all the Templar Knights were well-known as knights of God.

Another thought struck her. Was he praying for the men that had lost their lives? Was he praying for her father? A heavy guilt descended over her. She should be doing the same. It couldn't hurt. But she had not been raised in any faith or belief. The only things she trusted were the edge of a blade and her family. Still, saying quiet words or a simple goodbye might be fitting.

What would it accomplish? Angrily, she turned away from the chapel. There had to be justice for her father's murder. She was going to make sure of it.

She walked down the hallway. Landyn wouldn't give her any information, so she needed to talk to someone who would know about the mission and the men who had attacked. She would speak with the Templar in charge of the chateau. The commander.

Landyn always felt better after praying. His mind was clearer and more focused. He had asked for guidance with Raven.

The task of protecting her was something he didn't want any part of, especially because of her vow of revenge. Still, it was important to him to honor John's last wish. He planned to find her after speaking with the commander and discuss her plans.

As he approached the commander's working room, he heard two voices and recognized both. Apprehension snaked through him.

"It is a great loss. I will miss him terribly." It was the commander's deep voice.

"Yes. He often spoke of your friendship," Raven said. "And how important that mission was to him. All those knights... I just wish I knew who had attacked them."

"It was the king's men. We didn't think they were that close. They must have been watching the chateau."

"And the man with the eye patch?"

Landyn hurried to step into the room...

But he was too late.

"Captain Pierre Boucher."

The commander looked up from behind his desk. His white hair and beard blended into his ivory tunic adorned with the red cross. His wrinkled hands were folded on the desk, and he leaned forward.

Raven twisted in the chair before the desk to lock gazes with Landyn. When her stare alighted on him, a guarded veil fell over her eyes before she looked back at the commander.

"Ahh, Landyn!" the commander called. "I wanted to speak to you. Come." He stood. "It has been a pleasure meeting you, Raven. My condolences for your father. We shall all miss him."

"Thank you," Raven replied solemnly.

As she walked past Landyn to exit the room, she gave him a triumphant glance. She now knew who had killed her father.

Landyn shook his head as she departed.

Once she was out of the room, the commander wondered, "You don't like her?"

Landyn eased the door closed and stepped up to the commander. "I don't trust her."

"Trust? She is Hawke's daughter. How can you say that?"

He took a deep breath. "John was a good friend. I trusted him. But Raven…" He peered at the door. "She wants revenge. Boucher killed her father."

The commander sat back in his chair, rubbing his beard thoughtfully. "Boucher led the men who attacked you?"

Landyn nodded.

"How is it you escaped the attack?"

"I was with Raven. John sent me to protect her." His lips tightened. "If I had been there… If I had been with John…"

"You would have been killed, too. He saved your life by sending you to protect his daughter."

Landyn shook his head in disagreement. He should have been with the Templar Knights. He should have been with John.

"The woman is headstrong, is she not?"

Landyn again glanced at the door and chuckled. "She is a Hawke."

The commander nodded knowingly. "I like her, too."

Landyn's eyebrows rose in surprise. He hadn't said he *liked* her.

"What will you do now?"

Landyn dropped his chin to his chest. He would do what he didn't want to do. "After I see Raven to safety, I have to go after Boucher. He has John's key."

The commander's eyes widened, and he leaned forward on the desk. "Does he know what it is for?"

"He knows as much as I do. But John insisted the key belonged to his daughters. He wanted me to get it back and give it to them."

"Boucher is leading his men toward La Rochelle and the nearby port."

Landyn looked away. That made sense. Boucher was trying to find the Templar treasure. Boucher and the king must have believed the Templar Knights were going to ship it away to a safe area. Landyn felt his fists clenching, and he purposely relaxed them. There had been a time when going after Boucher was the only thing he'd desired. He'd believed Boucher's death would appease him. But that was years ago. He still felt that hunger thriving in his heart. He was afraid if he pursued Boucher that the anger and darkness would return and consume him.

"Will you be able to do it?" the commander asked. "Will you be able to face him? To kill him?"

Landyn's teeth clenched. It was his old, instinctual reaction to Boucher. Hate. He took a deep breath, but before he could answer, the door swung open.

Raven entered. "I'll do it."

CHAPTER SEVEN

Landyn whirled on Raven and grabbed her arm in a firm grip as he spoke to the commander. "Please give us a moment."

He guided her out of the room and glared at her. "You can't go. You don't know what you're getting involved in."

"If my father wanted me to have the key, then I'm already involved," she responded, lifting her chin defiantly.

Landyn ground his teeth. She had clearly been listening in on the commander and his conversation. "It's dangerous, Raven. Boucher is merciless. He has committed atrocities."

"Like killing my father?"

"Worse. He is pure evil. He's the only man I know of who has no morals."

"Stop. You're scaring me," she said with thick sarcasm.

"I wish I were truly scaring you. There is no reason for you to do this. This is not what your father

80

would have wanted for you. Go to Sybil's farm. Find your sisters."

Raven's eyes narrowed; her blue eyes flashed. "Don't tell me what my father wanted."

Landyn's stern glare softened. She was hurting, he knew. "He was my friend, Raven. I will miss him, too."

Grief flashed in her eyes for a moment, like a fleeting raindrop. Then it was gone. "You won't miss him as much as I will." She spun and stepped into the room toward the commander.

Trouble, Landyn thought as he followed her. How could he keep his oath to take care of her if she insisted on risking her life?

The commander leaned back in his chair, surveying them with astute eyes.

"I will find him," Raven announced.

There was only one way to keep her safe. If he agreed to locate Boucher and return with the key, then there would be no reason for her to go. "She doesn't know how to get word back to you about her progress," he said to the commander. "I'll do it."

Her mouth dropped, and her gaze swung to him in shocked anger. "The commander can tell me," she argued.

"She isn't as experienced as I am tracking."

"How hard can it be to track a squadron?" she retorted.

"She is a woman," Landyn said, staring at the commander. He would say anything to get him to dismiss her.

Raven's eyes widened in outrage. "I can do anything he can do!"

"Except let this go," Landyn quipped.

"Enough," the commander said in a strict voice, silencing both of them. He leaned forward and clasped his hands on the desk. He looked at Raven. "I know of your reputation and skill with the sword." His gaze swung back and forth between Landyn and Raven. "This is a dangerous job. Both of you are capable of doing it alone. But it would be safer if you didn't."

Landyn grinned internally, satisfied. The commander was not going to let her go after Boucher.

"You shall work *together* to find Boucher and retrieve your father's key," the commander announced.

Raven's teeth ground as she walked through the corridors of the chateau toward the inner ward. Work together, she thought with disgust.

Landyn followed her.

She didn't look, but she could feel his obnoxious presence and hear his booted footfalls.

As they emerged into the inner ward, the stable boy rushed up to them. He spoke to Landyn. "Father Michel has organized the burial as ye requested."

Landyn patted the boy on the head. "Thank you. Please prepare our horses."

Will bobbed his head eagerly, locks of his brown moppy hair falling into his eyes. He brushed them aside and raced off toward the stables.

"You should say goodbye to your father," Landyn suggested.

Raven gritted her teeth. "I already have." She

continued toward the stables.

"I said those things to prevent you from coming," Landyn said, following her. "I didn't mean them."

"There is truth in even the smallest of lies."

He grabbed her arm, halting her. "I'm going to see my friend put to rest. We will leave after that."

Raven watched him walk toward the chapel in the rear of the chateau. She clenched her fists. He was not giving her orders. She would depart when she wanted. Glancing at the stables, she straightened. She could leave now; she didn't need him. The commander wasn't paying her, and he was not her superior. His order to work together meant nothing to her. And yet…

She hesitated. She could certainly track a large squadron; it wouldn't be hard. But it would be difficult to get close to Boucher and kill him let alone find this key her father wished her to have. She needed more information. How could she separate Boucher from his squadron? What was the key? What if she took the wrong one? And why had Boucher taken it?

And those crates still bothered her. What had been inside of them? She wanted to know what treasure was more important than the Templar Knights they'd lost. Then her father's life? She clenched her lips. She would wait for Landyn. He had all the answers. She wished Willow were here to make her smile and convince Landyn to tell them what they wanted to know. But she wasn't. And each moment Raven wasted was a moment her father's killer got farther away. She hoped to meet up with her sisters at Sybil's farm. But their disappearance was odd and concerning.

With a groan, she grudgingly followed Landyn to the chapel. He moved around to the rear of the large cathedral.

Raven looked up at the roof of the stone building where a bell was housed in a triangular structure. On top of this, there was a cross. It would have meant nothing to her father. He was not a religious man. She continued around to the back but halted suddenly.

A wooden box rested beside a rectangular hole in the ground. A monk in a brown robe stood over the hole, speaking quietly. Landyn stood beside him with his hands folded before him, his head bowed. A solemn group of men gathered around the grave and the coffin.

Raven couldn't remove her gaze from the hole. How had they dug it so quickly? It was strange her mind focused on the opening in the ground and not the box where her father's body lay. He would never like being put in the ground.

She rested her shoulder against the stone wall of the chapel to watch. She didn't want to move closer. She didn't want to enter the yard where all the dead people were.

The monk made the sign of the cross, and all the men followed his lead.

Her father had never been a religious man. They never spoke of his beliefs or God. He didn't take them to mass. The only time Raven had been to church was when she was staying with Sybil. She remembered asking her father once what happened after you died. He looked at her pensively and replied, "Life goes on."

The group of men picked up the box reverently.

Raven's heart tightened and constricted as they lowered it into the hole. Life didn't go on for the dead, she thought sadly. When the coffin — when her *father* — was in the grave and no longer visible, Raven returned to the stables.

Will, the stable boy, greeted her at the door and handed Thunder's reins to her. She cast him a small smile before opening a pouch at her belt and pulling out a shilling. She handed it to him. "You've done a fine job caring for him," she told the boy.

He beamed proudly, staring at the coin in his hand.

"Care for my sisters' horses," she told him.

"I will!" he exclaimed and rushed into the stall of Sage's horse and began to comb him.

Raven grinned at the boy's exuberance and glanced at her horse. As she ran a hand over Thunder's brown nose, she noticed saddlebags had been added to her horse. She looked Thunder in the eye. "I'll make sure you get enough rest," she assured him quietly. Thunder had been a gift from her father. To teach her responsibility, he had said. She had learned to love Thunder as she cared for him.

She would miss her father. And for the first time, she realized just how alone she truly was. Usually, her sisters were around to pester her. But now, she didn't know where they were. She hoped they were at Sybil's farm. What was she to do now? The only things she could think of were to find Boucher, retrieve her father's key, and avenge his death.

"I thought you would have left." Landyn's

voice sounded behind her.

"In a few moments, I would have." She walked her horse from the stables.

Landyn followed with his horse and pulled himself into the saddle.

Raven mounted Thunder. She realized quickly that she didn't know where to start looking for the squadron. She knew they were heading toward La Rochelle but didn't know which way the army would have taken from Peniscola. She could backtrack, but that would take valuable time. Her fists tightened over the reins.

She needed Landyn to lead the way. She clenched her jaw. She certainly would not tell him that.

He steadied his anxious horse but didn't move it.

She sighed softly, keeping her gaze focused on the open gates. Oh, he knew. He knew she didn't know which way to go. He was purposely waiting. Raven didn't look back at him.

With a chuckle that grated her nerves, Landyn cantered his steed past her.

Of all the men to work with, why had the commander put them together? Raven wondered with aggravation.

Landyn and Raven rode quickly until the sun was beginning its downward path. He had been pleased to find she wasn't one of those travelers who needed to talk the entire time. Either that was the reason she was so silent, or she was still angry with what he had said. He hadn't meant his derogatory remark about her being a woman. She was probably as good at tracking and sword skills as some men he knew. But they needed to work together now.

They paused down the road from the village of Les Tiplies. The main road extended into the small town. Farmers' fields stretched behind the homes.

"If the squadron entered the town, the villagers would have knowledge of it," Landyn said, his gaze on the empty road leading into town and the wattle and daub houses at the entrance.

Raven hesitated, scanning the area. "We should stay out of the village."

Shocked, Landyn looked for the evidence she saw, but everything appeared normal to him. The road entering the town was open. Homes and businesses dotted the side of the street like in any other village. Nothing seemed out of place.

"We can find the information we need by asking the farmers on the outskirts," she suggested.

Landyn shook his head. "There is nothing wrong here."

"If a squadron of men came through harassing the villagers, the people will be unlikely to welcome strangers," Raven advised.

"There is no sign the squadron has been this way," Landyn insisted.

Raven grinned sarcastically. "Then why are we going this way?" She pointed to the village. "There are no people out. No animals. No children playing."

Landyn had to agree that was strange but not unheard of. "Perhaps they are eating or in for the night."

Raven cocked her head to the side in thought. "Perhaps. I'm going around the rear to speak with farmers," she stated. "If you're insisting on going into the town, be careful. Watch your back." She spurred her horse in an arc around the side of the houses. "I'll meet you at the end of the road, outside the village."

He clenched his teeth. He didn't like her going alone. Not when Boucher was out there. He spurred his horse after her and cut her off. "We shouldn't split up."

"I'm touched you're worried about me," she replied, her tone thick with sarcasm. "But I can take care of myself." She directed her horse around him.

Landyn watched her ride away. Stubborn, he told himself. But she was not Viola. She *could* take care of herself. "Be careful!" he called. After a moment, he steered his horse toward the village.

He trotted the steed down the dirt road, eyeing the surroundings. There were no people out. Not even children. No animals. It was as Raven had said. Usually, he wouldn't have thought too much about it, but since she'd pointed it out…

Tingles of unease spread up his spine. It *was* unusual. A breeze swept by him, and he slowed his steed to a walk, observing the houses for any indication of movement or occupancy. Even the bakery was closed. Perhaps that was normal for this town.

Perhaps it wasn't.

His senses were heightened. Leaves rustled. Birds chirped and flew through the sky. Yet, he saw no sign that a large group of men had been through this village. Not the destruction he would expect from Boucher. He spurred his horse. He didn't like leaving Raven alone, but this job was only going to be finished by sticking to the mission. Not traveling through back routes. If a squadron had been through this village or anywhere around, the villagers would know.

But where were the people?

He heard a scamper of footsteps and turned his head in time to see a young boy scurry behind a barrel near one home. He guided his steed over slowly. "I won't hurt you, boy."

No movement came from behind the barrel.

"I'm looking for a large group of men," Landyn said.

Silence for a lengthy moment.

Landyn wondered if the boy had heard him.

"Are you with 'em?" a tentative voice finally asked.

"No. I am Sir Landyn of Winchester. I am with the Templar Knights."

The boy poked his head out from behind the iron-bound wooden barrel, a lock of black hair falling into his eyes. "Where's yer white tunic?"

"I'm on a secret mission."

His gaze moved over Landyn, and he stepped from behind the barrel. He couldn't have been more than ten summers. "Can ya help us? I mean, if ye're with the Templars, ya have ta, right?"

"Help you with what?"

"Couple a men came into town. They took whatever they wanted without paying fer it. They took me da prisoner, forcing him ta work for them."

That sounded like Boucher. Landyn's jaw clenched. "Where are they?"

"I'll show ya." The boy ran up the dirt street.

Landyn followed, pushing his horse into a trot. One-story homes and businesses lined the street. Wooden signs hung outside of shops, describing them. Bakery. Candlemaker. Beside the blacksmith's shop was a two-story inn. The boy stopped before the door, pointing inside and hopping from foot to foot in excitement.

Landyn dismounted, tying the reins of his horse around a tree branch. He glanced at the door, his hand dropping to the hilt of his sword. "How many are inside the inn?"

"Two fighting men," the boy responded. "George, the innkeeper. Maggie and me da."

Landyn took a breath and reached for the handle of the door. He pushed it open.

The main room was lit by a low burning hearth, casting a red pallor over the room. Two doors flanked the hearth on the opposite wall. A couple of black-tunicked men sat at a large table in the center of the room. They looked up when Landyn entered.

The boy's father must be working behind one of the doors, Landyn thought.

The child scurried past him into the main room.

Landyn reached out to stop him, but he hurried by. He must be going to help his father, even though it was dangerous. Landyn closed the door behind him as the two men rose from the table. "Where is the boy's father?" he demanded.

The boy paused at one of the black-tunicked men's sides. He gazed up at the one with long, dark hair. "I done good, didn't I?"

Landyn scowled in confusion.

The man handed the boy a coin and pushed him

aside before drawing his sword, chuckling. "You did good."

What was going on? Landyn slowly eased his sword from the sheath. Two untrained men would be no problem for him. Afterwards, he would figure out why the boy had led him here.

Suddenly, the doors on the opposite wall opened. Two men with black tunics emerged from one door, and two men with the king's heraldry on their tunics came out of the other door. Four more men.

A trap!

CHAPTER EIGHT

Raven's gaze skimmed the farmland, looking for clues like tracks in the dirt. A squadron wouldn't be able to move through the countryside without leaving something behind. Horse manure, at the very least. Unless they didn't come this way or were trying to remain hidden.

She took her time, trying to use her skills. She knew how to track. Her father had trained her and her sisters. She recalled one time when she was young; they were tracking a path their father had left for them, and Willow had been distracted chasing a butterfly. She was the only one not to follow the track that day. Their father had not been happy.

Now, they were all skilled trackers. She and Sage often made a competition of it.

Tracking a squadron shouldn't be this difficult. Where had they camped?

She stared out at the horizon between the trees lining the farmer's field. A large grassy area was just beyond the trees in the distance.

She spurred her horse forward, easing him along the edges of the pasture. She was certain the crops had already been collected, but she didn't want to risk angering the farmer. When she reached the field, she stopped.

Some of the tall stalks of grass had been flattened. Piles of ash from campfires dotted the field.

This was what she expected to see if a large group of men had come this way. She grinned, pleased, and turned her steed toward the town.

A stocky farmer had emerged from one of the houses, and when he saw her, he quickly turned back into his home, closing the door behind him.

The villagers were frightened — the men had not treated them well. She ground her teeth. Power and strength did not make it right to mistreat those weaker than you. She urged her horse into a gallop, her body moving with ease and the familiarity of Thunder's gait. She stopped before the farmer's house and dismounted. She knocked on the door. "I'm sorry to disturb you," she called through the door. "I want to know more about the men that camped in the field."

"Go away!" a male voice called from inside.

Raven shook her head. Willow was always better at speaking with people than she was. But there was one thing everyone understood. Her hand wrapped around her coin purse on her belt. "I will pay for your time."

There was silence. Raven glanced around at the other farm homes. Perhaps she could locate someone else more willing to speak to her.

The door cracked open, revealing a tiny sliver

of darkness. "We want no trouble," the voice from inside said.

"I'm not with those men. I'm sorry for the way they treated you."

Whispers sounded from inside the home. Then, the man's voice. "How much are you going to pay?"

Raven sighed softly and opened a pouch tied to her belt. She removed a shilling and held it up.

After a moment, a hand extended, palm up.

Raven pulled the coin back. "First, answer my questions." She rubbed the coin between her fingers. "How long did the group stay?"

"A night," the farmer answered.

"When did they arrive?"

"Yesterday. 'N they ate all our crops. Drank our ale. And paid nothin' fer it."

"When did they leave?"

"Leave?" he echoed. "Four of 'em are still at the inn."

Dread clawed its way up her spine. "Where is the inn?"

"Next to the blacksmith's shop." He stretched out his hand.

Raven dropped the shilling into his palm and put her booted foot into the stirrup to mount.

"Best be careful," he advised. "There are also two of the king's men at the inn. They arrived early this morn."

"Thank you." She spurred her horse and rode between the farmer's home to the main road. She hurried, looking for the blacksmith's shop.

Landyn was in trouble.

Landyn blocked the swing of the first man with the long, dark hair. The others were coming toward him, drawing their weapons. He had to get out of there. The king's men must be there because Boucher's men were passing on information about the crates to them.

He parried another blow from the dark-haired man when a second male with a scar across his cheek stepped forward, lunging his blade in low. Landyn swung to deflect the second man's strike. Both of these men had been at the table when he arrived.

In his peripheral vision, he saw the king's men approaching.

As the long-haired man raised his sword, Landyn kicked him back and lunged into the scarred man. Landyn's blade pierced his stomach, but he didn't have time to watch the man with the scar fall. He pulled his sword free and twisted out of the way of another swing from a third male with a scraggly beard.

He couldn't defeat five armed men.

The clangs rang through the room. In the hearth, sparks jumped and snapped.

Landyn engaged the scraggly bearded man with a flurry of quick attacks. He had a better chance of defeating him now before the long-haired man got to his feet. But the bearded man deflected all his blows.

The last black-tunicked man with cropped brown hair helped the long-haired man to his feet.

As they joined the fight, Landyn backed behind a table, separating himself from the three black-tunicked men. He glanced over the room. He was battling Boucher's thugs, but the king's men were approaching behind them. His hand gripped the handle of his sword tightly, and his breathing came in even gasps. Five men.

The man with the beard jerked to go around the table to Landyn's right, and Landyn stepped back, but not far enough that the man with the cropped hair on Landyn's left could strike. The man with the long hair grabbed the edge of the wooden table and tossed it aside.

Landyn threw a chair at the cropped-haired man and parried an attack from the man with the beard. He acted on instinct but was hard-pressed to defend himself against three men. If the king's men joined the battle, he would have no chance. He had to defeat them before the king's men joined in. He swung and blocked and struck and deflected. Twisting and turning and constantly moving away from the black-tunicked attackers. He tried to head toward the door, hoping he could get out of the room, but the bearded man stepped into his path.

He pulled back, twirling to lock swords with the cropped-haired man. He seized his wrist and whirled him around, throwing him into the long-haired man. They collided and fell into a pile on the floor.

One of the king's men rushed toward him, his sword raised above his head.

Landyn dodged the blow and elbowed the man in the face. He turned in time to block a swing from the bearded man.

The king's man grabbed Landyn around the neck, ordering, "Finish him!"

The bearded man knocked Landyn's sword aside, sending it flying across the room to land with a clang somewhere on the floor. Then, the bearded man pulled his arm back to run Landyn through.

Landyn grasped the arm about his neck and twisted to the side.

The bearded man impaled the king's man.

When the king's man's grip loosened, Landyn broke free, throwing a punch into the bearded man's chin.

The long-haired man came up behind him and grasped a handful of Landyn's hair. He shoved Landyn's face into the wall.

Landyn's head rebounded against the wood. His world spun.

The long-haired man tossed him across the room into one of the tables.

Landyn landed hard on the wooden surface, and it collapsed around him, sending him and some mugs crashing to the floor. His vision swam, but he attempted to scan the ground around him for his weapon. He blinked, struggling to clear his foggy mind. Splinters of wood surrounded him as well as broken shards of mugs. He couldn't find his sword.

A shadow fell over him, and he turned back. He shook his head, trying to free himself from the stupor.

The long-haired man stood over him, grimacing. He spat blood to the side.

Landyn tried to shift backward but could barely lift himself. He attempted to kick the long-haired man, but the man caught Landyn's foot and tossed it aside as if it were a limp rag.

The long-haired man raised his sword above his

head, the tip aiming down.

The flames from the hearth flickered.

Landyn stared at the long-haired man standing over him. Was this how his life ended? Was this the man who ended it? A feeble, untrained thug? He wouldn't get to finish his oath to John and protect Raven. Strange that in his last moments, he would think of her. The man's sword appeared frozen in the air. Why wasn't Boucher's man bringing the blade down? What was he waiting for?

Red liquid dribbled from the corner of the long-haired man's mouth. As the sound of familiar tings rang through the air, the long-haired man toppled forward like a tree.

Landyn was barely able to move out of the way as Boucher's man landed beside him. The long-haired man sprawled next to him, face down and unmoving. Confused, Landyn eased himself to a sitting position. A red bloom spread across the back of the man's black tunic.

The tings continued around him, and he looked up.

It was like a dream. It didn't seem real. Raven blocked a strike from the king's man, the only man standing. All of Boucher's thugs lay on the ground.

Landyn shook his head, trying to comprehend. Was he dead? How could this be happening?

He watched the swordfight for a moment through a narrow tunnel of vision. Raven moved with grace, dodging the swings of the king's man. She was a small target, and she was quick. Her motions were like a dance. She ducked one swing and lunged in, catching the king's man in his side, where he wore no chainmail armor.

She was good.

She pulled her sword free, and the king's man clutched his side, staring at her in shock before dropping to his knees and finally to the ground.

She was very good.

She glanced around the room, grasping her sword. Thin, shapely, confident. She looked like a Greek goddess of war, beautiful with death all around her. Then she locked eyes with him.

Landyn's world spun. It was as though a bolt of lightning shot through him.

Raven had saved his life.

CHAPTER NINE

Raven knelt at Landyn's side, inspecting his face, her gaze sweeping over every inch of his skin. From the nasty-looking lump on his forehead, down over his full lips and chin covered by a day's growth of beard. He appeared unharmed, except for a red welt on his head. She sighed in relief. "You're going to have a bump on your forehead."

He nodded and put a hand to his injury. He attempted to stand but had to grip the back of a chair to steady himself.

Raven reached out to grasp his arm.

"My sword," Landyn said, searching for it on the floor.

She skimmed the wooden pieces of the table on the ground for it. Finally, she spotted a sword across the room and rose, walking to the corner. She picked up the blade. "My father always said if you lose your weapon, you're dead." She displayed the sword to him, questioning if it was his.

Landyn rubbed his head. "Good advice."

Raven handed the weapon to him, and he sheathed it. She gazed at the dead bodies on the floor. Two of them wore the heraldry of the king. The rest were the men that had attacked the Templar caravan. "Boucher and his men came through the town. I found their campsite and spoke with a farmer."

Landyn nodded again. "Search these men. Take what you can."

A woman with dark hair and a concerned, fearful look in her eyes peeked out from one of the doors.

Raven glanced at the carnage and the broken table. This fight would be costly to the owners. "Leave them," she suggested. "Let the innkeeper keep what he can find."

Landyn agreed with a nod.

Raven was beginning to like the bump on his head; she liked that he couldn't argue with her. Or perhaps he actually agreed with her. That would be a stunning victory. "Can you ride?"

"Of course," he said. He wobbled slightly.

He could barely stand; there was no way he could ride. She would have to find somewhere to rest for the night. She took a step and waited for him to do the same.

He did and began falling sideways.

Raven caught him by the waist to balance him, and her fingers spanned his middle. He had hard muscle and planes beneath his black tunic. Her stare shifted to his eyes, where she found them closed, strands of his dark hair swept forward. The bump on his head was rising.

She remembered a time she and Sage had been

arguing. Sage had hit her over the head with a wooden sword, and Raven had been so dizzy that she had to sit down until nightfall. Oh, Raven had made Sage pay for that. She had pretended to be so shaky she couldn't do anything. Sage had made her dinner, cleaned up, and even covered her with a blanket for the night. Sage had felt so guilty.

Raven wrapped an arm about Landyn's waist and placed his arm over her shoulder. "We'll walk." She helped him to the door, pretending not to notice how much he leaned on her. She grasped the handle and opened the door.

"You're good," he said quietly.

"What?" she asked as they emerged into the setting sun.

"Your sword skills are excellent."

A satisfied grin fell over her lips. "You had already taken out two of them."

"And you took out four."

Her horse stood beside his black steed. She reached for his animal's reins without releasing Landyn. "I had a great teacher."

He swayed and almost fell, but she steadied him.

"You can't ride," she stated.

He inhaled a deep breath, expanding his already broad chest. "No. I don't believe I can."

Raven scanned the landscape, checking to see if anyone was watching them or if there was a safe place to stop. She didn't want to return to the squadron's campsite in case some of Boucher's men were lurking around. She didn't want to risk being ambushed. She glanced at Landyn. He was in no shape to fight — he needed to rest.

"We'll walk down the road and find somewhere to stop for the night," she stated.

Raven stopped walking when the moon had risen, and trees lined the street. She led the horses and helped Landyn through the trees to a small, open area. Sheltered by a canopy of treetops, the area was mostly dirt, fallen branches, and an occasional weed. It was far enough from the road that no one would see them, yet close enough to a small stream that the horses could drink.

Landyn sat beneath a tall tree as she tied the horses' reins to a branch of a tree near the stream. Then, she ran her hand along Thunder's neck before moving to the saddlebags filled with supplies the monks had given them. She removed a flask and some food and returned to Landyn's side to sit. Unwrapping the cloth around the food, she handed him cheese and bread. "How do you feel?"

"Better, now that we are resting," he admitted.

She took a bite of the cheese and eyed his injury. "You have a lump on your forehead."

Landyn lifted his hand and drew his fingers along his brow. He found it immediately. "It's nothing."

Raven retrieved a small pouch from her horse's saddlebags. "Let me see it."

Another sigh from Landyn.

She knelt before him, examining the bump. "My father used to come back from jobs often with bruises and cuts." She moved her hand toward him. He tensed. "We were all trained how to care for sword wounds." She gently ran her fingertips along his forehead, encircling the bump to see if it was hot. He relaxed beneath her touch. "Willow is the best at caring for injuries, but we can all do it. She is the most compassionate."

"You're not compassionate?" he scoffed. "I find that hard to believe."

She raised an eyebrow and purposely pressed against the bump.

"Ow!" He pulled back.

She nodded. "You just need time. A cool cloth will help, but there's not more I can do." She sat back on her heels. "Any other injuries?"

"Not that I know of."

"Take your tunic off," she commanded, opening the pouch.

He hesitated.

She peered at him with a sarcastic twist of her lips. "I can't see through your tunic. Don't worry." She grinned and joked, "I promise not to fall in love with you."

That did it. He unbuckled his belt, put it aside, and lifted the tunic over his head.

Raven had often seen her father's upper body when he was working, practicing with his sword, or injured. But she rarely saw another man's torso. And she had definitely never seen one like Landyn's. His torso was sculpted and powerful. She swallowed heavily, staring.

"Do you see any cuts?" he asked.

She cleared her throat and looked away. "No. Nothing. No cuts." She couldn't resist a glance back at his amazing body. His arm muscles rippled as he reached for his tunic. The planes on his stomach clenched as he raised it above his head to pull it down. For a moment, Raven was disappointed she couldn't watch any longer.

She mentally shook herself and gathered her pouch. As she was going to stand, he grasped her wrist.

"What about you?" he wondered.

"What about me?" she asked.

"Do you have any injuries?"

Outrage filled her. "I'm not taking my armor off!"

He chuckled softly, and the ripples warmed and relaxed her. "No," he said. "Were you hurt during the fight?"

"No," she replied and stood. "Not even a cut. I do know how to sword fight."

"So do I," he protested. "But there were a lot of them."

She felt she should appease his ego. "I caught them by surprise. They were too interested in you to notice me. I had taken down two of them before they knew what was happening." She uncorked the flask and took a long drink, the soothing ale washing down her dry throat. She handed the flask to him. "What were the king's men doing there?"

Landyn swallowed a drink of the ale as Raven pulled the cloth open around her food. When he finished, he glanced at her. "Perchance Boucher's men were reporting to them. He is the king's lackey."

"They must have wanted what was in those crates." She leaned forward slightly. "The *treasure*."

Landyn locked gazes with her.

She really had no clue whether there had been

treasure in those crates or whether Boucher had gotten it or not. She tried to gage Landyn, but his face remained void of reaction. She tightened her jaw, realizing he saw through her bluff. "What was in those crates?"

Landyn rubbed his head and shook it. "Nothing."

"I know. I saw the empty crates. I'm speaking about before Boucher took whatever was in them. Was it treasure?"

Landyn sighed softly and lay back. "We should get some rest. We haven't slept in almost a day."

"The key my father spoke of. The key that belongs to me and my sisters. What does it open?"

"I honestly don't know. But it was important to John that you have it."

Why? Raven chewed her lip. This was a mystery that Sage would love. It just annoyed Raven. Everything about this entire situation was irritating. She stood, angered that he wouldn't tell her what was in the crates. Angry that she had to find a key she knew nothing about. Angry that her father was gone.

And worried.

She forced herself not to think of her missing sisters. Not now. First, she would seek revenge on the man that killed her father. Then she would meet them back at Sybil's farm. They would be there. They had to be there.

She whirled and stalked across the small clearing to another tree to sit.

"Thank you."

She almost didn't hear the words. She spun on him. "What?" she snapped.

"Thank you," Landyn repeated. "For saving my life."

She stood, stunned. Then she nodded in acceptance of his gratitude. "You're welcome."

"You were right. The men didn't come through the town. But some of them had remained behind. There was a boy who said his father needed help. They ambushed me."

"Why?" It made no sense. Why would they ambush him?

"Boucher's army consists of mercenaries. They must have thought to gain more coin by robbing merchants and getting free meals. They used the boy to lure travelers to the inn where they could rob them."

Raven shook her head in disgust. Those poor villagers had no chance of standing against the mercenaries. A sword in the wrong hands was dangerous. "At least they won't bother anyone again."

Landyn settled back against the tree.

Raven crossed her legs and sat down. The only thing that mattered was Boucher. And how his life would end because of what he did to her father.

"You must be careful of this man. Boucher is dangerous. He has no code. No loyalty."

"The king would not deal with a man like that."

"If it fit his purpose, he would. Boucher has worked for the king for a long time. He has always done distasteful jobs for him."

"How do you know so much about him?" Raven wondered suspiciously. When Landyn remained silent, she asked, "Have you met him?"

"He was the reason I am joining the Templar

Knights."

Surprise shot through Raven. "So, you know him. What happened?"

He glanced at her with haunted eyes and then closed them. "Get some rest."

She wondered what Boucher could have done to Landyn that was extreme enough to make him join the Templar Knights. "He won't be alive to harm anyone anymore."

Silence settled around them, and Raven fell into a deep sleep, replaying the death of her father over and over in her mind as she cascaded into darkness.

Landyn woke with a horrible headache, shooting pain pulsing just behind his forehead. He sat up slowly and found the clearing empty. He looked for Raven as he sluggishly stood, but he couldn't see her. The gaps in the trees didn't yield any sight of her. Perhaps she had gone to tend to the horses near the stream? He made his way through the brush, stepping over a branch and strolling through the leaves to the stream. As he approached the gently rushing water, he spotted her bent over at the edge. Her feet were bare, her boots at her side. She leaned toward the water.

He trod on a twig, rustling leaves as he walked.

She whirled, shooting to her feet. When she saw him, her eyes widened, and her hands darted behind her back as if hiding something. Her hair was wet and hung in long dark locks over her shoulders.

He registered all of this, but his eyes shifted to her unlaced leather armor and the dark chemise she wore beneath. Both hung about her smooth shoulders. Her chemise dipped precariously low over her chest, revealing the delectable swells of her breasts.

They stood that way for a moment before Landyn was able to tear his gaze from her provocative curves. "What are you doing?"

"Nothing," she said defensively.

He glanced at the stream behind her and then back. It was obvious she was washing. It wasn't a sin. In fact, it was admirable.

"I mean…" She indicated the water with a flick of her hand while keeping the other behind her back. "Rinsing the dust off."

"What's behind your back?"

She delicately chewed her lower lip. "Nothing of importance."

"Then show it to me."

"You don't need to know."

He still didn't trust her. Was it a dagger she was sharpening? Was it some kind of poison she was mixing?

And then his gaze dropped to her chest again. Was it some potion to entice him? He didn't believe in magic or witchcraft, but some plants were known to have lust-inducing properties. His gaze locked with hers. "Show me."

Her jaw stiffened, and her lips thinned. "Fine. Fine. If you must know." She presented a small pottery jar with a cork in it. "Satisfied?"

"What is it?"

She shook it before him, and liquid sloshed inside. "A jar," she said mockingly.

"What's inside?" Poison came to mind again.

She hesitated, her gaze sweeping the trees behind him as if searching for an answer.

He held out his hand. "Give it to me."

"No," she snapped, drawing it to her chest and holding it protectively. "It's mine."

"What is it?" he demanded.

Raven sighed and rolled her eyes. "Willow made it for me. It's rose water."

He scowled in confusion.

"To make my hair smell good," she clarified, as if to a simpleton.

He still didn't understand. "Why were you hiding it?"

She dropped her gaze to the ground and stroked the pottery jar with her finger. "I don't do things like this. I don't care if my cheeks are red. I don't care if my hair is a mess." She looked up at him. "But I like the way my hair smells when I use this."

Landyn stared at her, trying to hide a smile. Her beautiful blue eyes were vulnerable and conflicted. It was a simple joy. One that hurt no one. He would never fault her for it. In fact, he thought it made her more attractive. More precious. More beautiful if that was possible.

His eyes swept over her smooth, bare shoulders one last luscious time.

"So now you know my secret. Are you happy?" she asked.

"It is nothing to be embarrassed about. I respect you for it."

She straightened. "You do?"

"It is a simple pleasure. There is nothing wrong with it."

110

She grinned in satisfaction and bowed her chin shyly.

"I'll wait for you in camp," he said, backing away. But he couldn't take his gaze from her. She looked like a seductive water nymph, standing at the edge of the stream with her wet hair hanging about her shoulders. He bet it smelled just like roses and, for a moment, longed to test this theory.

He tripped on a branch but caught his balance and spun, returning to the camp.

Raven's fingers moved through her wet hair quickly, braiding it tightly at the back of her head. She grinned as she recalled Landyn's acceptance of her rose water. She had expected him to critique her, to make fun of her.

But he hadn't.

It must be his bump, she thought. It had done something to his mind. Made him a more likeable man. She righted her chemise and tied her leather armor closed at the front of her body.

Man — the word echoed in her mind as a softly calling siren. She recalled the firmness of his torso, the muscled perfection of his chest and arms. She sighed softly.

Thunder nickered.

She cast him a glance. "Don't judge me," she warned.

Something had changed between her and Landyn, and she wasn't sure what it was. But she liked it.

Landyn allowed Raven to take the lead as they rode because he was in no mood for tracking. His head still pounded beneath the warm rays of the morning sun. Raven was an excellent tracker, picking up Boucher and his men's path numerous times when Landyn thought they had lost it. They were heading north. He knew their destination. La Rochelle. The squadron had gone off the main road and was heading toward the Ruisseau de Granes. The river.

Boucher was approximately half a day's ride before them.

With the sun high over their heads, Raven stopped at the edge of the river to rest the horses.

Landyn watched her swing her leg over her saddle to dismount. His eyes lingered on her rounded bottom before her feet hit the ground, and he tore his gaze away. The image of her bare shoulders and wet hair still lingered in his mind. He was a man, after all. Still, it was inappropriate and disrespectful to John to think of his daughter that way.

He had to contemplate something else. Boucher. The thought of him always sent anger through Landyn, no matter how much he tried to dismiss it. And now, the same rage burned in Raven. He wished he could convince her to give up seeking Boucher's death, that there was so much more to life than violent vengeance. "Why is it easier for you to go after your father's killer than to find your sisters?" he asked her as he climbed from the saddle.

Raven's hand froze in midair. She had been

about to tie the reins of her horse to a nearby tree. Then, her hand lowered, and she slowly turned to him.

"Aren't you worried about them?" he asked. "I mean, one of them was with Brother Nicolas, and he was found dead."

"Of course, I'm worried about them. But I won't let my father's murderer escape without punishment," she replied and swung the reins around a tree branch.

"Your sisters could be in danger."

She put her hand on her hip and faced him. "Do you have any siblings?"

"No," he replied. "But if I did, I would find them. The living are more important than the dead."

She thought about his statement before speaking. "We were all trained to take care of ourselves. But yes. I'm worried about my sisters. They are my only remaining family." She took a step closer to him. "I don't know where they are, and I don't know how to find them. My only recourse is to hunt my father's killer. It serves two purposes." She held up her pointer finger. "Revenge for killing my father." She held up her middle finger to indicate second. "And if my sisters are in trouble, and I kill Boucher, it will send a message to whoever is endangering them: I will hunt them if they harm my family."

Landyn stared into her determined eyes. It was sound thinking. He understood the message she wanted to send to others, but he didn't agree with pursuing vengeance.

She cocked her head to the side. "Where is your family? Where are your parents?"

"Both have passed."

"Then you have no family."

He rose to his full height. "My Templar brothers are my family."

Her gaze traversed him from head to foot, and she lifted an eyebrow.

He didn't like the look she bestowed upon him. "They are family even if we are not bound by blood," he insisted. "I would do anything for them. Just as your father did."

Confusion flashed in her blue eyes, and she scowled. "What do you mean by that? My father had a family, and it wasn't the Templars."

Landyn led his horse to the river. "John respected the traditions and the ways of the Templars. He was incredibly loyal to them. In fact, he wanted to be a Templar Knight. John was the one who convinced me to become a Templar, to serve the order."

Raven's frown deepened, and she stepped up beside him.

"We were good friends," Landyn said, remembering. "Your father was a strong man. He was proud of you girls and loved you very much." He looked at her. "You were the reason he gave up becoming a Templar Knight."

CHAPTER TEN

Raven's skin tingled as shock scorched through her. Had her father wanted to be a Templar Knight? "But he never... He never spoke of the Templars. He never said anything."

"He wouldn't have," Landyn claimed. "He kept it separate from you."

Raven shook her head in confusion.

"You know this area well, yes?" Landyn asked.

Raven glanced around at the surrounding river and trees. "Well, not this specific spot. But the roads and villages around..." What had the land to do with her father? "My father worked jobs around here. We know the area well, yes."

"And you never wondered why? Or what jobs he was working? Or for whom?"

"Of course, I did. But he wouldn't tell me who he was employed by. Finally, I stopped asking."

"He did many tasks for the Templars. He always helped them whenever they needed him. They would repay him with food for you girls."

Then Raven remembered the wagon of food he would return to Sybil's farm with. It would be stocked with meats and vegetables and cheeses. They would feast for days after he returned. The memory only brought realization and sadness. Her gaze slowly dropped to the ground. "Why wouldn't he have told us about wanting to become a Templar?"

"Because nothing was more important than you. He never regretted giving it up. He told me so. He told me you girls were the biggest treasures in his life."

Her chest tightened. She turned away to shield it from him. Why had her father never told her? She had to hear of her father's desires from another person. Her heart squeezed in her chest.

"He wouldn't want you to risk your life to avenge him," Landyn murmured.

She scowled fiercely, hearing the words but not agreeing with them. "He would do the same for us."

"He would never endanger any of you."

"I'm not endangering anyone."

"You are endangering yourself," Landyn insisted. "This is a dark path, Raven. One I would not wish on anyone."

"It's not your path," she asserted. "It is something *I* have to do." A thought struck her. "Don't Templars have a vow of chastity?"

"Aye."

"But my father and my mother… He had been with my mother at least three times. He said he loved her."

"Aye. That was why he had not joined the order sooner. He did love your mother. And he labored hard to support his family. That's why he was rarely home when you were young. He took job after job. You never wanted for anything. And then your mother passed, and he had the three of you to care for."

She and her sisters had taken away his dream. He had to watch them, so he couldn't pursue it. She wrapped her arms around her stomach.

"He gave you everything he could, Raven," Landyn said softly. "He would not have changed a thing."

"Except he would have become a Templar Knight," she whispered.

Landyn shook his head. "More than that, he wanted you to live a long life. That was what all the training was for. To prepare you for this moment. When he was gone."

Raven bowed her head. Her lips shivered. "I didn't know him," she whispered.

Landyn grabbed her wrist and tugged her against him, holding her.

She resisted at first, stiffening her body. But he squeezed her tightly. The warmth of his hard body soothed her, and she finally melted against him, letting his touch comfort her. He stroked her back with calming hands. She leaned her head against his shoulder. Her vision of the forest blurred as tears entered her eyes.

"You knew him," Landyn reassured her. "Just because you didn't know one thing about him doesn't mean you didn't know him. He was your father. You are more like him than you know."

Raven missed her father terribly. She missed his guidance, his leadership, his confidence.

Landyn hugged her close.

Memories of her father flooded her mind. The image of him standing with crossed arms, gazing at her with pride as she came back from her first hunt with a rabbit. His grinning visage as he watched all of them sharpening their swords. "I remember when my mother first passed, the Chateau le Bezu was the first place he took us. I remember how frightened Sage and Willow were."

"He knew many of the monks and knights there. He probably believed they could help."

She scoffed. "He didn't know what to do with us. Three girls. He didn't know how to raise three girls." She lifted her head from his shoulder and stepped back. "He was all we had."

"You still have your sisters."

Yes, but she didn't know where they were. Deep down, she was afraid to go to Sybil's farm. What if they weren't there? Her jaw tightened. She had to focus on Boucher. The image of Boucher stabbing her father as the others held him burned in her mind. What if her sisters were at Sybil's farm? How could she face them and tell them she couldn't save their father?

Landyn appeared to follow her train of thought. "If you murder your father's killer, then you become a killer."

"I don't have an option," she said softly.

"You always have an option. Think about it. Killing him with hatred in your heart will change you from the person you are into someone you don't want to be."

A shiver of trepidation snaked up her back. Was she doing the right thing? She lifted her gaze to him, struck by the truth in his words. She should have saved her father. And she couldn't do that. The next best thing was killing Boucher. She had no other choice. At least then she could face her sisters.

Tracking Boucher and his men was not as easy as Landyn would have thought. Raven believed they had split up at one point, and it took her time to find their trail again. Finally, she picked up the tracks just past a small hill.

By the time the sun was setting, Landyn and Raven agreed Boucher and his men couldn't be more than a day's ride before them because of the time it took to pick up the trail. They were hoping to catch up with them on the morrow. Now, they needed to conserve their strength and prepare for the confrontation. They rested for the night in a thick, grassy area.

Landyn lounged back against a boulder, stretching his feet out before him. He gazed at the darkening sky and wondered, "What did your family do when your father didn't have a job?"

Raven shrugged. "We started a warm fire and sang songs."

Landyn tilted his head and scowled at her in doubt. "Really?"

"No." She gestured at her horse with a wave of her hand. "We saw to our horses. Sharpened our weapons. Practiced."

Landyn settled back again. "You never spoke about your future… a family? Children?"

"We *are* a family. Children? I don't think any of

us have actually considered it. Did *you* think of children?"

Landyn sighed softly. He stared at the cloudless, colorful sky, but he didn't really see it. "There was a time, yes, when I thought of having children." Out of the corner of his eye, he saw her eyes round, and her brows raise.

"Were you married?"

"Yes," he replied. Immediately, he saw Viola's kind smile in his mind's eye. But most of the features of her face were fading. He just recalled her kindness. It always made him sad because, while that was her best quality, it had been her downfall. She had let the monster into their home.

"What happened?"

Landyn bowed his head, and his jaw clenched.

"Did you leave her?" Raven asked.

"Never," he ground out.

"Did she leave you?"

"No," he whispered.

"Did she die?"

"She was murdered."

Silence settled around them. The crickets chirped "don't tell her. Don't tell her."

The quiet was almost too much to bear. He felt compelled to say something. To explain what had happened, even though he didn't want to. "It was a long time ago," he said, trying to brush the topic away.

"Were they robbers?"

He sighed, knowing she wouldn't let it go. "Yes." His lips thinned. "It was robbers." The moment came back to him immediately, even though he had attempted to bury it previously. "She was in our home. The sun was high overhead. I was in the fields. Too far away to hear the horses' approach. I heard her screams. I ran back. But I couldn't save her." He clenched his jaw, remembering how he had found her on the floor in a pool of blood. "They wanted my sword."

"They?"

Landyn nodded and swallowed in a thick throat. Her chilling cries haunted his dreams every night. "Two men. They could have just taken it. They didn't need to kill her. I heard their laughter and saw them leaving our cottage as I got there."

"I'm sorry," Raven whispered.

How many times had he heard that over the years? But it had not made up for the uselessness he felt, nor the guilt and sorrow that burrowed into his heart. "It was a long time ago," he repeated. The pain was muted but never, ever forgotten.

"Did you kill the men who murdered her?"

Landyn felt his entire body clench. "No. I later found out that one died in a fight."

"You didn't go after them?" Raven asked, shocked.

He *had* gone after them. The need to kill them had consumed him for months. It was all he thought of; all he wanted. It had nearly killed him. And then he had met John at an inn. John had saved him. "I let it go."

"But they killed your wife." Raven shook her head. "I couldn't do that. I can't."

"You think you can't. You're not where I was. And I hope you never get there." He remembered the anger and the hate. It was like a disease inside of him. He lived in darkness and loathed his existence.

"What was her name?"

"Viola."

"That's a pretty name. What did she look like?"

He glanced at Raven. She was nothing like Raven. Viola wasn't a fighter. "She had brown hair that she liked to pull up off her shoulders. She used to say it was easier to work without it getting in the way. She was the kindest person I've ever met." He looked down at something poking him in the side and picked up a small twig. He twirled it in his fingers and caught Raven watching him from where she sat across from him. She had flattened the stalks of grass around her so she could sit. He grinned. "Her hair was lighter than yours. And her eyes were not as large." His gaze moved over Raven slowly. Raven was very beautiful. She was tiny but curvy in all the right places. And fierce.

"Did you love her?"

"More than life itself." He focused on Raven. "What of you? Have you ever been in love?"

Raven scoffed. "I never had time for love. Between practicing and making sure my sisters were following Father's orders, there was no time."

Sympathy flooded through Landyn. A beautiful woman like Raven had never known love. He scowled in disapproval. He was certain part of the blame lay with John. John would never have let men court his daughters. He trained them as fighters, not to be ladies. Landyn wondered what Raven would do if he kissed her. The thought sent a mischievous grin across his lips.

She straightened under his perusal. "What are you looking at?"

He smiled to himself. He had to admit it had

been a long time since he had kissed a woman. And Raven was very attractive, her lips full and inviting. Someone should kiss her. And kiss her well. "I can't imagine that men didn't try to kiss you."

"They didn't. Well…" She rolled her eyes. "There was a farmer's son once. But I shoved him down, and he never tried again."

Landyn chuckled.

"Are you offering?"

Her teasing question caught him off guard. "Would you let me?" he countered. After a moment of silence that challenged his future Templar oath, he quickly added, "I'd be afraid you would shove me down."

She snickered. "You're too strong. I don't think I'd be able to." She held up her hand. "It's well. I'm not asking you to kiss me."

A shame. He couldn't do it because of his future oath, but it was a shame, nonetheless.

A seductive grin curved her lips and sent his blood boiling. "I'd hate to be a temptation to your chastity oath," she said slyly.

She was toying with him. He ground his teeth and shifted his position lest she saw exactly how tempting he thought she was. He wasn't a Templar yet.

Silence settled around them. The ribbit of frogs singing, the calling of crickets, the constant humming of the forest lulled Landyn to peaceful rest, and he closed his eyes.

"Do you still remember her murder?" Raven asked quietly after an extended pause.

"Every day. Every day I see her blood on the wooden floor, and I remember. You won't forget."

"You shouldn't. You should never forget what they did to her."

Landyn was silent. No matter how much he tried, he couldn't stop seeing Viola's body on the floor.

"Did you ever get your sword back?" Raven asked.

"No. I never saw it again."

"They took your sword from you as Boucher took my father's life from me. I wish I had been there to defend him."

It wasn't quite the same, except both incidents ended in a loss of life. Landyn sat up. "His death is not your fault, Raven. Boucher would have attacked whether you were there or not. If his death is anyone's fault, it's mine. I should have stayed with John. In truth, the only life you saved by being there was mine."

Raven looked down, considering his words. Then she shifted her gaze to look at him beneath her lashes. "Then I am glad I was there."

An immediate pulse of arousal beat through him. The expression she bestowed on him was sultry and sensual. He couldn't stop staring at her full lips.

She grinned gently. "I guess that's two times I've saved your life."

Landyn slowly nodded in agreement. Now, he just needed to save hers.

CHAPTER ELEVEN

Later that night, something caused Raven to open her eyes. She sat up, always trusting her instincts. Her gaze immediately shifted to the spot where Landyn had been resting. Beneath the soft moonlight, she saw the flattened grass where he had slept, but it was empty. His blanket was crumpled where his feet had rested.

Raven looked around. The moon cast long shadows through the clearing and about the trees.

She heard soft grunts echoing through the air and tilted her head to listen. The noises stopped and were silent for a moment before starting again. Slowly, she stood and followed the sound through the small space where they rested to a clearing just beyond a line of trees. Fenced by tall trees, the moonlight created a pale glow over a circular grassy area.

Landyn stood in the middle, like a god of old. He clutched his sword; his arm muscles bunched tight. The moonlight gently caressed his shirtless torso like liquid gold, and his skin gleamed beneath its touch.

Raven pressed herself against the trunk of a tree to watch him in secret.

His chest heaved with his breathing as he faced his imaginary foe. Then he exploded in a barrage of swings and lunges, hacking at his invisible nemesis.

Raven found it difficult to believe he had ever been a farmer. He was made to be a warrior. His strikes were perfect, his form exact. His body, amazing. She could tell exactly where he imagined his foe standing. Each thrust struck the invisible torso. His arm muscles rippled with each swipe, and the planes of his chest and stomach tightened and released with force. His strength took her breath away. She heavily swallowed as she gazed in admiration. Suddenly, the thought of being kissed by him didn't seem so silly. Warmth spread through her as she imagined being wrapped in his power, being caressed by his fingers.

She softly sighed.

He whirled, the tip of his sword pointing at her.

They locked eyes for a long moment.

Raven had never been afraid of anything in her life. But the feelings that coursed through her now were terrifying. She wanted to step forward and push her lips to his. She wanted to touch his smooth stomach. She wanted to feel his hands on her. Instead, she stood, rooted to the ground.

He lowered his sword. They stared at each other for a long moment.

His black hair hung forward over his face, concealing his features in the darkness. Shadow and moonlight accented every curve of his body, highlighting every spectacular muscle he had.

Raven couldn't catch her breath. She couldn't speak. She couldn't think.

Landyn dropped his sword and stalked across the space between them. With a firm grip, he gathered her against him and lowered his head, claiming her lips, pressing his to hers hungrily.

Sensation exploded inside her as if every one of her senses were suddenly awakened. His hands tightened around her back, pulling her close. Heat radiated from him. He smelled of maleness and a musty, earthy scent. His breathing was quick and urgent. His lips moved demandingly over hers in an intense massage, coaxing her lips to part.

She was shocked at her own eager response and returned his kiss with reckless abandon. She opened her lips to his exploration, and he swept his tongue into her mouth. His kiss was as the soldering heat blacksmiths forged metal with.

A groan sprang from the very depths of her soul. Blood pounded through her veins, leapt from her heart, and made her knees weak.

He cupped the back of her head, anchoring her.

Her hands brushed up his muscled torso. His body was hot and slick and so hard. Everywhere she touched was rigged and planed with strength. Burning desire and an aching need for more scorched through in her.

Suddenly, he stepped back, releasing her.

Raven almost stumbled but righted herself and gazed at him with large eyes. Her heart pounded. She gaped at him, so handsome...

He took a step away from her.

The distance allowed fresh air to sweep in

between them and cool her body. What was wrong with her?

He cleared his throat before finally asking in a hoarse voice, "You couldn't sleep?"

Lord, what was happening? She wasn't the kind of woman to be swept off her feet. She was rational and… She licked her lips. "I heard…" She couldn't tear her gaze away from his lips. Those lips had kissed her. "Something."

His gaze shifted to the forest behind her. "I'll look around to make sure no one is here." When he turned back to her, his smoldering eyes locked with hers. "Go back to camp," he commanded and returned to the clearing. He picked up his sword and tunic and continued by her.

Raven watched him for a moment and noticed his rounded bottom for the first time. She leaned back against the tree with a silent groan. Her insides melted and swirled, and her mind fogged.

What was wrong with her? She traced her kiss-swollen lips with her fingers. He had told her to go back to camp. Why hadn't she argued? She wasn't a defenseless damsel to be ordered around. *Go back to camp.*

And yet, she looked at the path he had taken. He was so handsome. She could barely argue when he stared at her with those eyes. And his hair was so thick and wavy. All she wanted to do was run her fingers through it.

And his kiss. She inhaled slowly, deeply, closing her eyes to remember his moist caress.

She ground her teeth and mentally shook herself. This forest must be enchanted. There was no other logical reason for her reaction. She took a deep breath and pushed herself from the tree to return to camp.

He had kissed her.

Raven awoke to find Landyn across from her. He had finally fallen asleep. She had a moment to examine his peaceful face. He slept on his side with his arm tucked beneath his head. His jaw was square and strong and stubbled with morning's growth. A straight nose lined the center of his face. Long, thick lashes rested against his cheek. His hair crowned his head in a layer of dark waves.

He was handsome; she would give him that. And after the night before, she knew he was strong and muscled and…knew how to kiss. She grinned and again touched her lips, recalling Landyn's heated caress.

She inhaled a deep breath and closed her eyes, imagining Landyn's touch, the feel of his skin beneath her hands, the way he had ignited her body with his kiss.

She snapped her eyes open. This was dangerous—she couldn't like him. Focus, she told herself. She had to get her father's key back and deal with the man who had killed him.

She moved to the spot she slept in and picked up her sheath, silently sliding her sword free, glancing at Landyn to make sure the soft hiss hadn't woken him. She had just enough time to care for her sword before they continued tracking Boucher. She inspected the blade for knicks or breaks from the fight. Its surface was smooth and sturdy.

Removing a cloth from her saddlebag, she ran it over the edge.

A rustling caused her to lift her gaze to see Landyn sitting up and watching her. Heat inflamed her, and she quickly looked down at her sword again.

He traversed the area and took a seat beside her, crossing his legs. He held his sword in his hand.

She glanced at it. The metal gleamed in the morning sun. "How is your head?"

"Well," he answered. He withdrew a cloth from his bag and pushed it over his sword.

She stared at his silver blade. She knew she should say something about their kiss. They should talk about it. She should tell him that it didn't mean anything. But the only words she could find were, "That is a fine weapon."

"It does what it should. But it is nothing compared to my first one."

"Your first sword?" she asked.

"The one that was stolen." He rubbed the cloth along the edge, cleaning it. "It was made of Damascus steel. It was beautiful." He grinned and lifted his gaze to her.

Her heart did a little flip.

"Perfectly balanced and sharper than any sword I've seen," he continued.

The tender way his lips formed each word as he spoke captivated her. She couldn't tear her eyes from his lips.

"The grip was wrapped with alternating colors of leathers. But the pommel…" He inhaled in awe. "The pommel had a ruby the color of a rose, inlaid with an elaborate metal scrollwork surrounding it."

His finger traced the remembered details.

She gazed at his strong face, his black eyes, the way his dark hair caressed his shoulders.

He raised his stare from his weapon to her. "And what of your sword?"

"My sword?" Raven asked, having forgotten that she held it.

He reached out and tapped the metal blade. "This one. Where did you get it?"

She shifted her focus to her sword. It was safer than looking at him. "Father gave it to me. We each received a real sword when we turned ten summers. I remember the day I got it. We all had wooden swords first." She looked at him. "For practice." Her gaze traveled to his lips. Again. They settled there for a moment until she dragged her stare to her weapon. "When he gave it to me, he said there were three rules. Never use it against family. Care for it. And only use it if you can win."

"Wise rules," Landyn said.

Raven scrubbed the cloth over the blade. "I suppose a weapon is much like a kiss."

"Raven," Landyn said with a sigh.

"You don't have to worry. I just want you to know that I don't expect anything. It was a one-time kiss." The silence stretched, and she moved the cloth back and forth over the metal. She felt his intense stare on her and peered up at him.

"You didn't push me away," he said softly.

Her heart melted. "Did you expect me to?"

"No," he admitted honestly. "I just...I couldn't stop myself. When I saw you standing there..."

Raven shook her head. "We are working a job together. That's all. I don't expect to be kissed

131

again." There. She had said it. She had given him an escape. He was going to be a Templar Knight. He didn't need her to be his temptation. She cleaned her blade, rubbing off all the dirt.

He swept the cloth over his blade. "How is a weapon like a kiss?"

Raven examined her blade, holding it up so she could see any dents. "Well, you never kiss family passionately. You have to be careful who you kiss." She stood up, putting her hand on her hip. She grinned broadly at him. "And you only use a kiss if you can win." She turned to Thunder.

Landyn stood. "Did you win?"

"It's not *if* I won, but *what* I won." She grinned. "My first kiss." And it had been spectacular.

CHAPTER TWELVE

They weren't far behind Boucher. The squadron didn't move as fast as two people on horseback could. Tension knotted Landyn's shoulders at the thought. He felt the stirring of old anger and hatred; Landyn still wanted Boucher to pay for what he'd done to Viola. Landyn had thought he let all his rage and focus go, but apparently, it had festered inside of him. He needed to find something else to hold onto rather than vengeance. He cast a glance at Raven as she rode beside him.

He could tell she had reworked her hair into the braid because the locks that had caressed her cheeks yesterday were now gone. Something was different after their kiss. No matter how much he didn't want to admit it, he sensed her presence now like a warm breeze. He saw her, not as a friend's daughter, but as a woman. And that was trouble. He needed to stay focused on the mission. While John had asked Landyn to care for her, his upcoming oath to the Templar Knights loomed. Landyn was conflicted.

There was a war inside of him. So many reasons to stay away from her and guard his feelings.

He peered slyly at her. Her back was straight, her black braid trailing down to the saddle and swinging gently from side to side. Her fingers gripped the reins confidently.

An admiring grin slid over his lips. She was like a sweet piece of chocolate. An irresistible temptation.

"Look," Raven said and pointed to the rise of a hilltop.

His eyes followed her gesture, and he noticed a wooden cottage at the top of the hill. Fields of harvested farmland stretched around it.

She studied the ground. "It seems like some of the squad broke off and went there," she added.

Landyn looked at the road and confirmed there were horses' hoofprints heading up the hill. "For provisions, most likely," he said, and tingles raced along his spine as he observed the building. "We'll check if the farmers are well."

Raven glanced at him.

His stare centered on the wooden home. He didn't like the apprehensive feeling sweeping over him. He wasn't certain if the unease was because it reminded him so much of Viola and his home or if it was something else.

He urged his horse forward cautiously. His gaze traversed the landscape as he and Raven rode up. Then he peered back at the cottage. The fields were empty, and there was no sign of anything amiss. Still, he had this feeling in the pit of his stomach that something wasn't right. He just couldn't place what it was.

"No animals," Raven observed.

That was it. No horses in the back, no oxen. Not even a dog. He slowed his horse to a stop outside the cottage and dismounted, his hand moving to the pommel of his sword. A cool breeze blew by him, ruffling his hair. A browned leaf tumbled past. The door creaked open.

Landyn heard Raven dismount as he approached the door. He didn't want to frighten the farmer, but he didn't think it wise to call out. As he neared the door, something caught his attention around the side of the cottage. It looked like red on the ground, mixed with the brown soil. He approached cautiously; his hand tightened over the handle of his weapon.

He studied the red stain on the ground, and it seemed to be coming from…

He turned the corner and stopped. A shaggy mongrel dog lay on its side, its tongue hanging from his mouth. Blood pooled around the animal from a wound at his side.

Landyn raised his gaze, scanning the horizon. No other men were in sight across the fields. Boucher must have gotten what he wanted and left.

He turned to Raven. Boucher's presence didn't bode well for the farmers, as it hadn't for him. He returned to the door. "I don't think they're here any longer."

"Are they alive?" she asked, indicating the blood.

Landyn shook his head. "It was a dog."

"They killed a dog?" Raven asked in horrified disgust. She reached for the handle of the door. "Where are the farmers?"

Landyn caught her wrist, his jaw clenching. He slid his sword from its sheath. "Remember what I told you. Boucher has no morals. He takes what he wants and leaves death in his wake."

Raven peered at him, troubled.

His lips thinned as he looked at the door. He reached for the wooden panels and slowly eased the door open. It took a moment before his eyes adjusted to the darkness. In his mind, he saw a different home. His body tensed as the memories came flooding back. He saw feet hidden by the wooden frame of the door. He crept into the room. His booted foot stepped into something slick and made a sloshing sound as he pulled away. Blood.

A man slouched at the side of the door. Landyn perused his body to find a sword wound in the center of the man's torso.

Landyn's tense body relaxed. It was a man. A farmer. Not a woman. Not Viola. He walked by the unmoving man. Flies buzzed eagerly around the home.

Three mugs were on the table next to full bowls of porridge.

Landyn swung his gaze around the room. Behind the wooden table, he saw a skirt on the floor. He froze as memories of Viola flooded his mind. He'd thought he had rid himself of the beast of those memories. The horror, the sorrow. But everything came rushing back. Every emotion. He blinked, thinking he imagined the familiar scene. He stiffly rounded the table. The woman lay on her back, her eyes open and staring at him. "Landyn," she called in his mind. He stumbled away.

Then he realized it was not Viola. The grief

overwhelmed him. He feared he was losing his mind.

"She must have been protecting him," Raven observed.

Landyn began to shake. While the woman on the floor was not Viola, his wife was all he could see. His failure to protect her clawed at him.

"Landyn," Raven whispered and brushed by him.

He jumped as she bumped him, swiveling to her.

She moved around the woman to another body huddled behind her. The corpse was lost in oversized clothing. Raven bent beside it, peeling aside the fabric. The face of a boy came into view.

Landyn's gaze swung back to the woman. Her child. Her boy.

Overwhelming grief pierced his chest. His breathing deepened, and his eyes burned. The room closed in on him, and he suddenly couldn't breathe. He whirled and fled the room.

The sun washed over him as he emerged from the house, but there was no warmth in its rays. He was cold. Shaking. He inhaled a trembling breath and ran his hands over his face, trying to regain his senses. It was too much. Too real. Too devastating. He'd thought he had buried those emotions. He knew they would never go away, but he hadn't known they were still that close to the surface, that raw.

As his breathing slowed, his jaw clenched. If he had stopped Boucher before, these people would still be alive. The realization hit him hard, and he stumbled back. He should not have sought Boucher for personal reasons, for vengeance. Landyn should have killed him for the other atrocities he would commit. The other lives he would take.

Landyn's jaw clenched.

"Are you well?" Raven asked.

Landyn whirled. She stood in the doorway, holding his sword.

She extended it to him. "You dropped your sword."

Glancing at the scabbard, he was shocked to find it empty. He hadn't even realized he had dropped it. He took another breath, retrieved it from her hand, and shoved it into its sheath but couldn't meet her eyes and instead skimmed the brown earth below their feet.

"Landyn," she said with concern and tenderness. "Are you well?"

"They need to be buried," he said. "I'll dig a grave." He turned away from her.

"Landyn," she called again.

He halted. His back was rigid, his muscles tense.

"It was Boucher, wasn't it?" she asked softly. "That killed your wife."

His shoulders drooped, and he hung his head. "Yes."

A long moment passed. Silence surrounded them. Finally, Raven said, "I'll prepare the farmers for burial."

Landyn knew it was time to rectify the mistake he had made. It was time to make it right and heal his soul. Boucher could not be allowed to kill defenseless farmers any longer. He had to be stopped.

Raven had taken blankets from the beds and rolled the farmer and his wife in separate ones. She lay the child flat on the final blanket — he couldn't have been more than five summers. She brushed his dirty brown hair from his closed eyes. His mother had fought to save him. She had found defensive wounds on the woman's hands and arms.

Raven folded a corner of the blanket over the boy's face and pulled the edges over his body. Landyn had repeatedly warned her that Boucher had no morals, but killing a child went beyond that. Boucher was a monster.

She stared down at the three blankets. These farmers shouldn't have died. They were defenseless against Boucher's sword.

Landyn's reaction had concerned her. She had known his wife was murdered. But had it been like this? And by Boucher. Her jaw clenched. They both had a reason for wanting the monster dead.

She glanced at the door. Landyn was taking a long time to dig the graves. Suspicion prickled the nape of her neck, and she went outside to check on him.

A cool breeze brushed her cheeks as she stepped out of the cottage. A shallow grave had been dug at the side of the house. She scanned the area for Landyn. She didn't see him. "Landyn?" she called.

Then, she noticed the horses were gone. Both Thunder and Landyn's steed. Her jaw clenched. Her fists balled.

He had taken Thunder and left her!

CHAPTER THIRTEEN

Just before sunset, Landyn lay in the tall grass of a hilltop overlooking a large group of men setting up camp for the night. Small campfires dotted the valley below him.

Boucher was somewhere in that camp. Landyn was close to finding him. It had been a long time since he wanted revenge. Now, it wasn't revenge as much as it was a necessity. For all those lives Boucher had slain, for all the people he would endanger if Landyn let him live. He hoped Raven would forgive him for leaving her. It was for her own good. He had to protect her. He had to do for her what he couldn't for Viola. He couldn't watch Boucher kill her.

Protecting her was essential because of his vow to John to take care of her. He tried to convince himself there was no other reason. It certainly couldn't be because of the way she looked at him. Nor the image of her lips and soft body or the feel of their kiss that still stirred his desire.

He slowly retreated from his hiding spot and returned to the horses he had left tethered in a nearby forest.

As he was riding away from the cottage, Raven's horse had pulled back, rearing onto its hind legs, tugging at the reins, and had almost unhorsed him. After a moment of defiance, the steed had continued with him. Landyn believed Raven had used that high whistle of hers to call the horse back. Landyn should have been prepared for that. But it hadn't changed his mind.

He rode for the rest of the day, tiring the horses out and finally catching up to Boucher's squadron.

He found them camped for the night in the valley below. His only obstacle now was to figure out where Boucher was and how to reach him.

His steed pulled at the tethered reins as he approached. Landyn ran a hand along his horse's nose and whispered calming words to soothe him. For some reason, the horse was nervous. They were far enough away that the men in the valley shouldn't be causing his horse anxiety. He patted the neck of his horse and stepped out from behind him. Raven's horse seemed relaxed as he ate some of the grass at his feet.

Suddenly, a man in a beige tunic was shoved to the ground at his feet.

Landyn recoiled, startled, and reached for the handle of his sword.

"You're getting careless," Raven said, stepping from behind a thick tree trunk. She gripped her sword tightly in her hand.

Shock blasted through him. How had she found

him?

"He's been following you since the farmer's cottage," she said, gesturing to the man cowering on the ground. Her tone was taut.

"How did you find me?" he asked in amazement.

She shoved the tip of her sword into the ground and stepped past him to her horse, spearing Landyn with a burning look of rage. She tugged open a saddlebag on her horse and pulled out a piece of rope before returning to the man on the ground. She yanked one of his hands behind his back. "Give me the other one," she commanded between her teeth.

The man grimaced but did not comply.

Landyn took a step forward to help Raven.

She grabbed the man's brown hair and yanked his head back. "You've been a pain in my arse all day. I'd love to slit your throat."

He groaned from an open mouth that had lost many teeth. He reluctantly put his hand behind his back.

She wrapped the rope around his wrists and pulled it tightly. Then she turned her full anger on Landyn. Like rays of fury, her eyes scorched him.

He almost recoiled beneath the weight of her rage.

She rose stiffly. Her hands balled into fists. "I should run you through."

The man on the ground lifted his gaze to look at Landyn in curiosity.

Landyn held up his hands in supplication. "I know you're angry —"

"You have no idea how angry," she snarled through clenched teeth. "You took Thunder."

"I had to take him. You would have followed me."

"I *still* followed you."

He was both impressed and annoyed that she had. He had underestimated her. "I had to take him. It was the only way to prevent you from following me. The only way to keep you safe," he admitted.

"Keep me safe?" she repeated in disgust. "I didn't ask you to do so. I don't need you to keep me safe."

"You think you don't, but you are wrong. You don't know Boucher. He is a dangerous man," Landyn protested.

"He is," the man on the ground agreed.

"Shut up," Raven snapped at the toothless man without taking her gaze from Landyn. "I don't care how dangerous he is. You left me."

"You should care!" Landyn hollered, his blood boiling at her innocence, her insistence. "About all of this."

"I don't care because I am more dangerous than he is."

"You think you are, but you're wrong."

"He killed my father," Raven growled with murderous rage clenching her jaw.

"I know he did. And he killed those farmers. But you are not like him. He is sneaky and murderous. And cold. And you are none of those things. He'll kill you just as he did those farmers."

"I am not one of those farmers. I'm trained to defend myself."

"She is good with a sword," the man on the ground agreed.

"Shut. Up!" Raven hollered more forcefully. She

marched up to Landyn.

"John was good with a sword, and Boucher killed him," Landyn said rationally.

Raven's glare turned furious, irrational. "This is my mission. *My* father was killed. You've given up every right to be part of it by leaving me."

Landyn shook his head. "I promised John I would care for you."

"And you do that by leaving me?"

"By protecting you."

Raven stepped up to him, pushing toward him. "I am not your wife. I don't need your protection."

The mention of Viola caught him unaware. He was certain she had done it on purpose, to stun him. He ground his teeth and swallowed in a tight throat. "Boucher doesn't play by the rules. If he hurt you… If he *killed* you… I don't know…"

"Don't know what?" she demanded.

Landyn's shoulders sagged. "I don't know what I would do."

"Because of your misguided vow to my father?" Raven challenged.

"Yes. No! Because of so much more. You're smart and beautiful and strong and talented. I couldn't risk your life."

"So instead of facing this together, you ran away? You left me alone."

Landyn clenched his teeth. "I was going to kill him so he couldn't hurt anyone else." His chin lowered to his chest, and he stared down at his feet. "I should have done it after he killed Viola. Then those farmers would still be alive. John would still be alive."

Her gaze raked over him, and her mouth closed

into a thin line. She suddenly pressed her lips to his.

Raven wanted to punish him. But she also wanted to console him. And she desperately wanted to kiss him. His lips were firm with shock for a moment. Then, they softened beneath hers like a sigh, and he took control. He answered her need with desperation and heat. His lips slid across hers in a moist, expert kiss.

She had been in control when it started, but suddenly as his hands wrapped around her, one entwining in her hair, her restraint swirled away in a flood of rising desire. He pushed tight against her, and she felt the length of his hard body. She had never wanted to be kissed before. But it was different with Landyn. She wanted to be in his arms; she wanted to feel him. It was a desperate need, almost as essential as breathing.

Her horse whinnied. It was an alarm in her mind, and she turned her head from Landyn's kiss out of instinct. Through a foggy awareness, she saw the captured man climbing to his feet.

As if a bucket of water were dumped over her heated skin, the passion was gone. She pulled away from Landyn, yanked her sword from the dirt, and dashed two steps after the man.

The man bowed his head and cringed from her as she reached him. "I was only stretching me feet," he said.

"On the ground," she ordered.

"But me feet—"

She lifted her sword to point it at his chest.

He nodded and dropped to his knees.

"On your stomach," Raven commanded.

The man took a deep breath and eased himself onto his stomach.

Raven glanced at Landyn.

He was closer and had his sword drawn.

She returned to his side, keeping an eye on their prisoner.

"What do you plan to do with him?" Landyn asked.

"Be merciful," the man pleaded. "I can help you."

"Tie him to that tree," she answered, indicating a nearby trunk with a jerk of her chin. "And gag him."

"Wait," Landyn called and walked past her to the man. He squatted down before him, examining him.

"Ya can't leave 'er in charge," the man argued. "I haven't seen the likes of her ever. She's abnormal."

Raven grabbed the man's arm and dragged him to his feet. "You're just upset because I beat you in a swordfight." She dragged him to the tree as Landyn stood.

"Ye're a girl! And ya cheated. There's no other reason ya could have beat me."

"There is one way." She pushed him down, leaning closer to him. "I'm better than you."

Landyn retrieved more rope from his saddlebag and brought it over to her.

Raven wrapped it around the man's torso and tied it in double knots behind him. She stood up, inspecting her work as Landyn placed a piece of cloth in the man's mouth and knotted it behind his head.

They stood and gazed down at the man. Raven released a sigh of satisfaction that the annoying man was finally gagged, and she wouldn't have to listen to his insults any longer.

She walked to her horse. Thunder nickered and pushed his nose into her shoulder. She stroked beneath his chin. "I've missed you too," she whispered and pressed a kiss to his nose. Instinctively, she began to inspect him, running her hand over the bridle and buckles on the saddle.

"I took good care of him," Landyn protested.

"You don't know him as I do," Raven answered. She picked up one of Thunder's front legs to inspect his hoof.

"I already did that."

She shot Landyn a scorching gaze before turning back to the hoof. She placed it on the ground and moved to Thunder's rear hoof.

Landyn sighed and walked to his horse to remove the flask from one of the bags. He uncorked it and drank deeply.

When Raven finished inspecting her horse, she looked at Landyn. He was watching her with the flask in his hand. She should be angry with him for leaving her. A breeze rippled strands of his black hair. He stared at her with an intensity that aroused her desire. She understood why he left her. It was wrong but reasonable.

Landyn offered her the flask.

Raven took it, grateful for the offer. She hadn't had anything to drink all day. She swallowed a mouthful. After her parched throat was satisfied, she lowered the flask and handed it back. As Landyn replaced it in his saddlebag, Raven said, "It's not your fault."

"What isn't?" Landyn asked.

"My father's death."

Landyn froze for a moment. Then he slowly turned to her.

"You couldn't have known what Boucher would do in the future. It's not your fault."

"It feels as if it is," he admitted.

Raven shrugged slightly. "My father always told us not to dwell on the past. You can't change it."

Landyn grinned. "That sounds like John." He lifted his dark eyes to her. "Why did you kiss me?"

Raven's cheeks burned, and it was her turn to glance away. She really had no idea. She had been angry with him. She had wanted to comfort him. But none of those reasons were the truth. She had wanted to connect with him again, wanted to feel his touch and caress.

He closed the distance between them and curved a finger beneath her chin, lifting her stare to meet his. "You know I'm planning to take a vow to the Templars. Nothing can happen between us."

Raven nodded. "I know." And yet, there was a stinging in her heart, and sadness fell over her like rain. What did she expect? That he would profess his eternal love for her? She mentally scoffed. She was not living a fantasy.

Landyn pivoted away.

She took a step after him. "Don't think that kiss meant forgiveness for leaving me. You're still in trouble for that."

He grinned. "I would expect no less."

She poked a finger into his chest. "Don't do it again."

He shrugged. "You'll just track me down. It's useless."

She agreed, satisfied. "A shame you didn't know that before you left me."

"How *did* you find me?"

She shrugged. "A farmer gave us a ride, and then we walked the rest of the way... It wasn't difficult."

The man tied to the tree grunted through the gag.

Raven and Landyn turned to him. Raven's gaze surveyed him. He was nothing but trouble, but her morals would not let her kill an unarmed man.

"What are you going to do with him?" Landyn asked.

She stared at the toothless man in contemplation for a moment. Cutting out his tongue for his disparaging remarks on the journey is what she wanted to do, but it would accomplish nothing. She couldn't set him free. He would return to Boucher and warn him.

The man grunted and struggled against his bonds.

Raven rolled her eyes. "I suppose, give him some ale. It was a long trip."

Landyn nodded. He removed the flask from his horse and walked to the man. He knelt beside him, slowly lowered his gag, and pressed the mouth of the flask to his lips, allowing him to drink. Then he lowered the flask and grabbed the gag to move it back into position.

"Wait!" the man pleaded, shifting his head so

Landyn couldn't put the gag on. "I can help you. I have no loyalty to Boucher."

Raven crossed her arms, unsure if she believed him. Mercenaries had loyalty only to coin. But Raven and Landyn certainly didn't have enough coin to pay more than Boucher.

Landyn yanked the gag over the man's mouth as the man protested, "I know where he is!"

CHAPTER FOURTEEN

Landyn paused and glanced at Raven. They locked gazes for a moment before he put the gag in the man's mouth and returned to Raven's side.

"Do you believe him?" Raven asked.

"Perchance," Landyn admitted. "Do you?"

"Not at all," she replied. "But we should listen to what he has to say."

"Agreed."

Together, they approached the man. His brown eyes swept from Landyn to Raven cautiously, and he pulled away from them.

Landyn stood over him. Why would his loyalty not be to Boucher? If he was a mercenary, which was mostly what Boucher's men comprised of, his loyalty was to coin. And Boucher was the one paying him. He knelt on one leg before the man and slipped the gag from his mouth. "Where is he?"

The man's stare rested on Raven and then shifted back to Landyn. "I must have yer word that ya won't kill me. That you'll set me free."

Raven bent toward him, her hands resting on her knees. "Or we can cut out your tongue."

"Raven," Landyn warned firmly before fixing his attention on the man. "We will set you free, unharmed, if you help us."

She straightened, crossing her arms. "It would have been easier to cut out his tongue."

The man scanned Landyn. "I take ya at yer word, Templar."

Landyn would never go back on his word. It was his oath.

"Boucher doesn't like to rest in a tent. He prefers an inn or farmhouse," the man explained.

Raven narrowed her eyes. "Why should we believe you?"

"Ya don't have to. I can prove it. I know where he is now."

"Where is he?" she demanded a little too eagerly.

"Go to the inn beyond the next town. He'll be there. The men camp outside of the town and meet him on the road the following day."

Landyn stood up. That would explain why some men broke off from the squadron and went to the last farmhouse. Landyn gritted his teeth. Finally. They knew where the murderer was.

"He likes to get what he can for free. If the owners aren't accommodating, he kills them."

Landyn clenched his lips. Boucher had to die. A man who cared so little for others' lives didn't deserve to be alive. He moved toward his horse.

"Are there any other men there?" Raven asked.

"He takes at least one man with him." The man's panicked stare followed Landyn. He struggled against his bonds. "I gave ya what ya wanted. Set me free!"

Raven marched to her horse. "We can't go charging in there."

Landyn tightened the strap on his horse's saddle. "We have to stop him before he kills anyone else."

"What about him?" Raven asked, jerking a chin at the man tied to the tree.

"We'll free him after we've killed Boucher."

"I gave ya what ya wanted!" the man protested. "Ya have to free me!"

Raven returned to the man's side. She positioned herself over him, staring down at him. "Is Boucher at the inn in Prat du Juge?"

He turned his head to the side defiantly. "I don't know. Free me and—"

Raven bent and seized his cheeks between her fingers. "Is he in Prat du Juge?" she demanded.

"Aye! Aye!"

She released him and straightened. Her jaw clenched tight.

"Now release me. Ya promised, Templar! Ya promised," the man begged. "What if Boucher kills ya? Then I'm stuck here."

Raven lifted the gag back into place over his mouth. "Pray he doesn't."

The moon was beginning to rise as they rode their horses to the inn. When the two-story wattle and daub building came into sight, they dismounted. Raven tied the reins of Landyn's horse to Thunder and slapped Thunder's rear. Her horse led Landyn's steed away toward a grassy area.

Raven stood at Landyn's side, gazing at the inn. Her insides clenched tight with concern.

"Are you well?" Landyn asked.

"I'm worried about the innkeeper," Raven said. She and her family had stopped here a handful of times. Rolf the innkeeper, his wife, and his boy were always kind and accommodating to her family. Rolf was an old warrior, and she liked him. He had married, settled here, and opened the inn.

She glanced at Landyn.

He nodded and shifted his gaze to the two-story wooden building. His jaw tensed, and his eyes fixated on the inn before he glanced at her. "I would prefer you wait here, but I know you won't."

She grinned. "No, I won't. You know I don't like being left alone."

"If anything happens —"

"Nothing will happen," she promised, yet trepidation swirled inside her. It was the type of unease that uncertain situations elicited in her.

His dark eyes swept her face in apprehension.

"You are stronger than you were," she comforted, needing to alleviate his fears as well as her own. "You have nothing to fear from him."

He turned to her and cupped her cheek. "Don't listen to anything he says. It's all lies."

She nodded. "Don't worry about me. I'll give you the first attempt at killing him. After that, it's my turn."

He chuckled softly and lowered his lips to hers in a soft, gentle kiss.

His kiss was moist and warm on her lips,

sparking a wave of yearning.

"I've never meant anyone like you," he whispered as he pulled away.

The kiss worried her. It felt like a goodbye kiss.

Landyn turned toward the inn and took a deep, cleansing breath. His entire demeanor changed. He straightened to his full height. His chin lowered and his lips curled. He became a warrior. A fighter.

As they approached the inn, Raven noticed three horses tied to a post at the back of the inn. Three horses? Had Boucher taken two men this time, or was the other horse from a traveler?

Landyn walked up to the door and eased it open, entering the main room. He stepped quietly into the room. Raven followed.

A dying fire in the hearth cast a red glow over the darkened area. Two wooden tables were in the center. Three mugs rested atop one of them. At this table, a man sat with his head on his arms. He wore a sword belted around his waist and a black tunic. One of Boucher's men.

Raven's gaze searched the rest of the room as Landyn walked up to the man. Another door was at the back, and a stairway led to the upper floor. She scanned the stairway with her eyes, but it was empty. The inn was silent. Too quiet. Her hand dropped to the pommel of her sword. Had they come in time to save Rolf and his family, or were they too late?

Landyn edged behind the man. He locked eyes with Raven and nodded.

"Rolf?" she called.

The dark-haired man on the table raised his head. He looked at her groggily, scanning her quickly before straightening in his chair and becoming more alert. He ran a hand across his crooked nose.

"Have you seen the innkeeper?" Raven asked. "His name is Rolf."

The man sneered. "All the rooms are taken. The innkeeper is not available. You'd best move on if you know what is good for ya."

Raven didn't like this man. Her jaw clenched, and her hand squeezed over the handle of her weapon. "Where is he?"

The man lowered his chin and stared at her with a threatening glare. "I told ya to *move on*." He put his palms on the table and began to rise.

Landyn slapped a hand on his shoulder and shoved him into his seat. He leaned forward to whisper in the man's ear, "Where is the innkeeper?"

The man's eyes shifted to the door. Then to Raven and his lip curled. "I don't know."

Landyn straightened. He indicated the door with a lift of his chin. "I'll take care of him."

Raven spun and hurried to the door. She eased the door open and waited for a moment as her eyes adjusted to the darkness. Slowly, she quietly slid her sword from its sheath and stepped into the room. The door swung closed behind her. A candle was lit on a wooden table in the center of the room, dripping wax down its slender form. A large hearth for cooking was against the back wall with a black cauldron in the center. The fire below the pot was extinguished.

Raven heard a shuffling of fabric and followed the sound to the corner. She gripped her sword tightly, preparing for a fight.

When she spotted a small shadow huddled behind a chair, she cautiously walked to the form, all the while scanning the room for others. When she stood before the shadow, two round eyes greeted her from the darkness.

A child.

Her heart twisted. The child was terrified. "It's well," she whispered. "I won't hurt you." She couldn't remember his name. "Where are your father and mother?"

"Upstairs," the boy uttered quietly. "In the last room."

Raven glanced toward the door. "How many men are there?"

"Three," the boy answered. "They told me ta wait here in case they needed anything."

"Stay here," she ordered. "Stay hidden, if you can." She turned toward the door. "I'll come for you when it's safe."

The boy's little hand darted out and caught her wrist. "Are ya going to save me mum and da?"

She nodded. "Aye."

Suddenly, the boy lurched forward and hugged her fiercely, frightened.

Shocked, Raven stood frozen for a moment. Then she sighed and squeezed the child. She patted his head. "Stay here." When the boy pulled back and hid behind the chair once again, she left the room, casting him one last look to make sure he was safe. He had disappeared into the darkness. She would not let them hurt him.

Murderers. Monsters.

When she emerged from the room, she spotted the man at the table lying the way he had when they entered, his head on the table. He was unmoving but she wasn't sure if he was dead. Either way, Landyn had taken care of him. But Landyn was not in the room. She lifted her gaze to the top of the stairs. It was the only place he would have disappeared to.

He was going after Boucher.

Landyn clutched his sword outside the first room. Boucher's man had not told him which room Boucher was in. And even if he had, Landyn wouldn't have believed him. He'd have to check every room. He came to the first door and paused, listening. No sound came from the room.

He clenched the handle and squeezed, opening the door a fraction so he could peer in. When the door squeaked, he froze, scanning the room for movement. It was dark, but he would see an outline or a shadow. Nothing moved. No animal, no person. He eased the door open farther.

Someone bumped his arm.

He jumped and whirled to find Raven standing behind him.

"This way," she whispered. She led the way down the hallway to the last door. She listened at the wooden frame for a moment.

Quiet sobbing came from inside the room.

Raven reached for the handle and pushed the door open.

A squeak of a floorboard alerted Landyn and he glanced over his shoulder. A man stood behind him, bringing down his sword.

Landyn acted quickly, pushing Raven into the

room away from the swing and lifting his blade to block the strike. The metal swords clanged as they came together.

The door closed behind Raven, sealing her in the room.

CHAPTER FIFTEEN

The glow of a candle on the tabletop beside the bed washed over the room in muted light and flickering shadow. A form sat up in the bed. A woman crouching on the floor didn't move, but the sobbing ceased.

Raven acted instinctively, lurching forward, and grabbed the woman's arm to yank her away from the bed, away from the man.

The woman's back arced, her hands clutching a black line around her throat. She fell to her knees, gagging.

Raven scanned the woman for the reason she was choking. She traced the black line around the woman's throat to the bed and the man. He had tied a rope around her neck to prevent her escape. He was choking her. Killing her. That was why she hadn't moved. He had a leash around her neck.

Raven brought the edge of her sword down on the rope, cutting it.

The woman fell forward to her hands and

knees, gasping.

Raven held her weapon out toward the man and put a hand on the woman's shoulder. "Are you well?" she asked with concern.

The woman nodded, her shoulders heaving as she slowly caught her breath.

Raven's furious gaze targeted the man who now stood at the side of the bed. His blond hair was in disarray, sticking up around his head. One of his eyes was gone. He still wore chainmail armor. "Go," she ordered the woman.

"Please," the woman gasped. "You have to help my husband."

"Where is he?"

"I'm not certain," she sobbed.

The man jerked forward as if to run past them out the door.

Raven stepped into his path, bringing the tip of her blade up. "Leave," she ordered the woman.

The woman quickly opened the door and fled, leaving the door open. Tings from a sword fight echoed in the hallway. Raven wanted to go to Landyn's aid, to help him, but she would not let Boucher go.

Flickering light from the torches in the corridor flooded the room. Raven's shadow fell over Boucher.

He smirked, stretching his hands out to the side. "I am weaponless. Surely, a woman of your honor would not strike me down without a weapon."

Her teeth ground, her body tensed with anger. He was mocking her. She held her sword out before her and approached him. "Did you give those unarmed farmers a fighting chance?" she asked in a low voice.

"Farmers?" His lip quivered in a grin. "Which ones?"

Fury fell over her. How many innocents had he killed? "Did you give my father a fighting chance?"

"Your father?" he asked in confusion.

"John Hawke."

"Ahhh!" His brows rose in understanding. "This is about revenge. Yes. I killed him as my men held him. He was weaponless; he didn't have a chance."

Raven's fist trembled as she gripped the sword.

"But killing me so coldly is not the Hawke way. You poor, pathetic people are *honorable*." He said the word with distaste. His smirk was dark.

He was right. Killing him outright was not the Hawke way. Although, she wanted to kill him for everything he had done to Rolf and his family, for the dead farmers, for Landyn's wife, and especially for her father. Her muscles quivered. "Where is my father's key?"

His lips turned up on one side. He knew he had the upper hand. He reached into his chainmail tunic and tugged out the key. It was on a black cord around his neck. "I like to keep mementos of my victories."

Raven forced herself to remain calm. He would not have that memento for long, she promised herself.

"Would you like a closer look at it?" He dangled it before him, swinging the golden key back and forth.

Her stare shifted from the key to his face. His bitter, laughing eye. "On your knees."

He hesitated.

She pointed the tip of the sword at his heart. She knew where to strike to wound him, regardless of the chainmail he wore. "On. Your. Knees," she repeated.

He reached out.

Wary of his intention, she backed a step away from him.

He grinned as he grasped the bed and lowered himself to his knees.

"Slide the key to me," she ordered.

He slowly bent forward to put the key on the ground. Then he shoved it. Hard. It glided across the room, away from her and toward the door. "Oops," he taunted.

Her gaze never wavered from him. He was not to be underestimated. At least he didn't have the key. She could look for it when he was dead. Her arm shook as she held her sword.

He had killed her father. Her father hadn't even been able to defend himself. Boucher had run him through.

Boucher glared at her from his kneeling position, his upper lip twisted into a grimace of loathing.

Her fingers convulsed over the handle of her weapon. It was time for him to die. It was time for her to avenge her father. She lifted her weapon over her head.

CHAPTER SIXTEEN

Raven's arms trembled as she held the sword above her head. Boucher had to die. To protect others from his evil. This monster would not hurt another family.

She heard Landyn's words in her mind, "If you murder your father's killer, then you become a killer."

While her heart was telling her to do it — to strike, to end his life — every other instinct she had prevented her from doing so. She was a Hawke; she did not kill defenseless men.

She was not a monster as he was.

With a frustrated growl, she lowered her weapon.

A sneer crept across his lips.

"Raven," Landyn called from the doorway.

She hesitated a moment, unable to face him. She was disheartened she couldn't finish the job.

Landyn moved up to her side. He placed a hand on her shoulder, which sagged beneath his touch.

"He killed my father," she whispered, her heart aching.

"I know."

"I can't do it," she admitted. "I can't kill him."

"I know." Landyn stepped up behind her and whispered against her ear, "Your father would be proud of you."

She looked down as tears rose in her eyes.

"This is yours now." Landyn held the corded key up at her side.

A simple gold key. She didn't know what it unlocked, but it now belonged to her as her father had wanted. She took the cord and slipped it over her head, tucking the key into her leather armor.

Disheartened, Raven took the rope from the bed and seized Boucher's arm, yanking it behind his back. She made sure she twisted his appendage just enough to cause him pain. She wrapped the twine around his wrist and secured it around his other wrist.

Then, she stepped before him. What was she going to do with him?

Landyn walked to Raven's side to stand before Boucher. "You have something that is mine." His gaze swept the room, searching.

Glinting in the soft candlelight beside Boucher's boots, it lay on a chair near the door. Landyn marched to the chair and picked it up.

His sword. The sword Boucher had killed Viola for.

"You," Boucher gasped. "I thought I recognized

you. The farmer. But no longer a farmer. Now a knight."

Landyn ignored him, inspecting his sword. He had half-expected Boucher to use it as an axe or treat it with disrespect. But it seemed remarkably well taken care of. There were no nicks in the metal blade, no rust. He ran his finger over the ruby in the pommel. Even it was intact.

"Where is it?" Boucher asked. "Where is the treasure?"

"You already know." Landyn turned away from him, moving toward Raven as he stared at his sword. The ruby in the pommel reflected the candlelight. Landyn ran his thumb reverently over the alternating colors of leather on the handle. He had thought he would never see his sword again.

Boucher's lips pursed and twisted in anger. "La Rochelle. You fooled all of us. I would have thought better of Templars."

Landyn met Raven's stare.

Pride and satisfaction shone in her bright blue eyes.

Boucher shook his head in disappointment. "It seems a waste to have killed her father for nothing."

Confusion flooded through Raven, sending tingles up her spine. What was this madman talking about?

"Oh, my dear," Boucher said, noticing her reaction. "You did know that the crates were empty, didn't you? It was a decoy. A ruse. A fake. I killed your father because those crates didn't hold the treasure we were after. They were empty."

Empty? She recalled seeing the crates open and empty, but there had never been any treasure? Her gaze swung to Landyn, pinning him to the spot. The caravan of Templar Knights, led by her father, were escorting worthless crates? Slowly, her brows came down over her eyes in a scowl of anger. "He died for nothing?" Her voice was tinged with hurt and disbelief.

Landyn put his palm up in supplication. "He did what he thought was right. It was important to him."

"You *knew*?" Her thoughts scrambled to understand his reasoning. "You knew the treasure wasn't in those crates?"

Landyn's shoulders sagged. "Aye."

"Why didn't you tell me?"

"I did. I told you nothing was in the crates, but I don't think you understood they were empty."

"Because it's irrational. Why would I understand?" she demanded. "Why would those crates be empty? Men died. My *father* died!"

"I...*we*...didn't think the king's men were that close." He jerked a thumb behind him, indicating Boucher. "We didn't think the king knew our plan."

"Your plan was to endanger all those men, to endanger my father, for nothing."

"Our plan was for them to follow us to the Peniscola port. By then, it would be too late to get to the treasure. They would have followed the wrong caravan." Landyn shook his head. "We were expecting an attack, but not of that magnitude. Not that early."

"The king was ready," Boucher interjected.

She shook her head. "Father died protecting a treasure that wasn't even there. His death was meaningless." A heavy sadness filled her, and her chest felt as if a thousand pounds were crushing it.

"He died so a corrupt king could not get his hands on the Templar treasure."

"Careful," Boucher warned. "That's treason."

"John died a hero," Landyn insisted.

Raven dropped her gaze to the floor, searching for the right answer. Searching for why her father had thought the treasure was so important—more important than his life. She took a step back. "You knew," she whispered again.

"Aye. I knew. But Raven—"

She held up a hand. "No. I...I don't understand. How could you have let him do that?"

Landyn paused, straightening in surprise. "*Let* him do it?" His body relaxed as if he had sighed. "It was John's idea," he said softly. "No one told John what to do." He dipped his chin and stared at her meaningfully. "He was a lot like you."

Her heart blossomed and softened at his words and gentle tone. He was right. Her father did what he wanted to, and no one told him otherwise. The fact that Landyn thought she was like her father sent waves of appreciation through her.

Movement behind Landyn drew her attention.

Boucher stood behind him, the rope dangling from his wrist, his hand pulled back with a dagger in his clenched fist.

"Landyn!" she cried.

CHAPTER SEVENTEEN

𝕴nstinctively, Landyn whirled at her cry, bringing his sword up and blocking the small dagger.

Boucher pulled back in angry surprise and lifted his hand for another strike.

Lunging forward, Landyn shoved his sword up beneath the chainmail shirt into Boucher's stomach.

The dagger froze in midair, and Boucher's hand trembled. His mouth hung open in disbelief.

Landyn yanked the sword free.

Boucher's fingers loosened, and the dagger dropped to the floor, landing with a dull clank. He toppled, grabbing hold of Landyn's shoulders, staring at him with horror.

"That's for all the defenseless people you killed," Landyn growled. He stepped back, shrugging free of Boucher's grip, and let him fall to the floor.

Time seemed to stop for a moment as Landyn stared down at Boucher. He lay on the wooden planks, face down. Landyn couldn't believe it was finally finished. All his days since Boucher had killed Viola had led to this moment. His hand squeezed the handle of his sword, now back with its rightful owner. It was only fitting that the first blood it tasted since being returned to him was the man who had taken it. A fulfilling tiredness eased through him.

Raven stepped up to Landyn, inspecting his torso with her eyes. Then, her fingers swept over him like little butterfly kisses. "Are you well? Did he cut you?"

"No," Landyn answered. He turned his full attention to her. "Raven, I'm sorry for not telling you —"

"You did," she replied, her hands lingering on his chest. "You have told me the truth since the first day I met you." She reached up to trail her fingers across his cheek. "About Boucher. About the treasure. About my father." She swiveled her face to look at him out of the corner of her eye. "There isn't anything else, is there?"

Landyn chuckled softly. "No." His gaze traveled down to her lips as if beckoned.

Suddenly, she stepped away from him and hurried into the hall. "Where's Rolf?"

"Don't worry. I found him tied in one of the rooms. The man guarding him is dead. Rolf is safe," Landyn said and brushed by her to lead her down the corridor. "This way." They rushed to the room with an open door.

Rolf sat on the bed, leaning forward, his head in his hands. His fingers moved over a old, ragged scar on his grizzled cheek. His gray hair was cut short, and he wore stained brown breeches and a tunic. His wife stood over him in a cream shift, rubbing his back.

The guard lay dead at his feet.

Empathy filled Landyn. He understood how Rolf felt. These mercenaries had invaded his inn, and he had been unable to defend and protect his family.

Raven's eyes widened. She squeezed Landyn's arm. "I'll be back."

He nodded, watching as she raced down the stairs. He walked into the room.

Rolf looked up with haunted eyes and rose. "I thank you for freeing my wife."

"It wasn't me. Raven freed her," Landyn replied.

"Raven?" Rolf asked, a scowl crossing his brow. "Hawke?"

Landyn nodded.

Rolf glanced toward the door. "Where is she?" he asked hopefully.

Landyn was amazed how her name could provoke such hope in the man. "You know her?"

Rolf nodded. "Aye. Her family occasionally stops here." His shoulders sagged. "I wish they had been here when these knaves arrived. They would never have allowed them to..."

"Father! Mother!" A boy raced into the room and embraced the woman.

Rolf's eyes brimmed with tears as he fell to his knees, hugging the two of them.

Raven entered after the boy. She grinned at the reunited family.

Landyn was so proud of her. So enamored with

her. So in love with her. She was everything to him. Everything. He never thought he would love again, and he had resisted it, resisted *her*, for so long. Somehow, she had snuck into his life, and now he did not want to spend a day without her.

Rolf rose, wiping a sleeve across his eyes. He strode to Raven and pulled her into a fierce bear hug. "Thank you for saving my family, Raven. Thank you."

She stood stiffly in his arms for a moment before melting into his embrace.

As Rolf returned to his family, Landyn and Raven stepped into the hallway. "What are we to do with the last mercenary?" Raven wondered to Landyn. "The one at the table in the main room?"

Landyn peered at Rolf, who lifted his head from embracing his family to hear their conversation. "Rolf can take him to the magistrate. He can dispense justice."

Rolf stared at him.

"Boucher's men will exact revenge on Rolf and his family when they find out Boucher was killed here," Raven whispered so the family would not hear her.

Landyn rubbed his jaw thoughtfully. "What else can we do?"

Rolf climbed to his feet and approached. "I'll get us some ale."

Landyn nodded and moved aside, watching him walk down the hallway. He glanced at Rolf's wife and son. She was speaking to the boy quietly, brushing tears from his cheeks.

"We can take the mercenary downstairs to a different magistrate," Raven suggested.

"It won't matter. The story will spread."

She lifted her hands helplessly. "There's also the mercenary we left tied in the forest."

"He won't tell anyone, particularly the squadron. If he did, he'd have to explain how *he* told us where to find Boucher. He'd be branded a traitor."

"We'll set that mercenary free."

Landyn nodded.

"In time," Raven said with a grin.

Landyn found himself smiling with her. Despite all they had been through, she was still able to entertain him. He looked back at the woman and her child. Slowly, his happiness faded. Boucher's darkness had touched another family. "Let's give them some time alone," he suggested and led the way down the stairs.

Raven followed him.

Landyn suddenly paused halfway to the main room.

Rolf stood behind the mercenary in the chair, gazing at him with clenched fists and hatred burning in his eyes.

The mercenary's head was still on the table as if he slept, but there was a dagger protruding from his back.

Raven halted, following Landyn's gaze.

Understanding and disappointment filled Landyn. He remembered the consuming sorrow and rage he had felt after Viola's murder. Landyn couldn't blame the innkeeper for killing the mercenary for what he had brought upon his family.

Rolf shifted his hard gaze to them. "It was the only way. The magistrate would do nothing about him. The vermin would tell the rest of the men, and me and my family would be punished." He spat on the dead man. "We've been punished enough."

Landyn cast Raven a glance. He lifted his eyebrows in resignation before continuing into the main room. He stopped across the table from Rolf, his gaze on the dead man. "Men from the squadron will still come here looking for Boucher," Landyn said.

Rolf nodded slowly, his lips thin. "I'll take this one far away from here and let the wolves have him. We'll tell the men we never saw Boucher. We'll tell them he never stopped at our inn. Lord knows I wish he hadn't."

Landyn hoped that would work. He hoped the innkeeper and his family would have no further trouble.

When Rolf looked at Raven and Landyn, his wrinkled face softened. "I can't thank you enough for what you did. He would have killed all of us. You saved us."

Landyn nodded in agreement and acceptance. He did not doubt Rolf was correct. Landyn was glad Boucher wouldn't be able to harm anyone ever again.

Landyn and Raven helped Rolf and his wife clean up. They loaded the bodies into Rolf's wagon. When they were finished, Rolf's wife made a warm porridge for them.

Raven finished the meal and glanced across the room toward Landyn. He towered over Rolf as he spoke to the old warrior.

Landyn had done what she couldn't. He had killed Boucher, avenging his wife, the farmers, and her father.

Disappointment welled within her. The code her father taught her and her sisters forbade them from killing a defenseless man. It was what made them different from these heartless mercenaries. However, that thought didn't ease her sense of remorse. She wished she could have gone through with it.

At least she had gotten her father's key back. She pulled it out of her armor and gazed at the gold key. Why had her fathered insisted she and her sisters have it? Why was it so important? She didn't know what it opened, and he hadn't given any clues. She stroked it with her thumb. It was the only thing she had of her father's—besides the traits he had instilled in them. She sighed softly. She would miss him dearly.

Landyn strolled over and took a seat across from her. He reached over the table and captured her hands in his. "Are you well?"

She squeezed his hands. "What if the squadron shows up here?" she wondered, glancing at Rolf. "Will they be safe?"

"Rolf will tell them he never saw Boucher." Landyn shrugged. "Without a leader, the men will either break up, or the king will appoint a new leader. I don't think they will cause trouble for him."

Raven nodded and tucked the key back into her armor. She sat back in her chair, studying Landyn. "What will you do now?" she asked hesitantly.

"Rolf insists we stay for the night while he

removes the bodies. He says it is the least he can do for us for saving his family."

"We have to free the mercenary we left tied to the tree," Raven said.

"We will." One side of his mouth moved up in a grin. "In the morning. There's no hurry. He'll be fine for the night."

Raven was satisfied with that answer. That man had insulted her the entire pursuit of Landyn. She would be happy to leave him gagged and tied to a tree for the night. She looked at Rolf. He stood over his wife, who sat in a chair holding their sleeping boy. He stroked her rumpled brown hair and pressed a kiss to the boy's head.

"What will you do now?" Landyn asked.

Raven stared at the family, and a longing opened in her heart. "I have to find my sisters," she said.

Landyn nodded. "We will."

"We?"

He lowered his chin and stared at her. "I gave my word."

Raven felt a twinge of discontent flip her stomach. He was still fulfilling his vow to her father. She had hoped he would help her because... Her shoulders sagged.

Because he wanted to be with her. Not because of some vow he'd made.

"We should rest," Landyn suggested. "We can discuss where to go from here in the morning."

Raven agreed. She was exhausted mentally and physically. She couldn't remember the last time she had gotten a full night's sleep. She glanced at Landyn and found him staring at her warmly. Heat flamed through her. And she wasn't certain she would sleep tonight.

CHAPTER EIGHTEEN

Rolf had given them separate rooms.

Raven tossed on her straw mattress. It wasn't that it was uncomfortable; she had slept in all sorts of locations that were not restful. Rather, it was knowing that Landyn was on the other side of the wall.

She gazed at the wooden planks where his room adjoined hers. The boards separating them were dusky without gaps. Was Landyn sleeping peacefully? Was he tossing? Was he thinking of her?

She crossed her arms in annoyance and pouted. Of course, he wasn't thinking of her! She was foolish to think he was. She was foolish even to *want* him to be thinking of her. He was going to become a Templar Knight. He couldn't be thinking of her. And yet...

She boosted herself onto her elbows. He was not a Templar Knight yet. He had not taken the vows. What if he *was* thinking of her? And she so desperately wanted to be with him. Just once to know what being held in his arms was like, what his body felt like.

Heat burned through her. And before she knew it, she was out of her bed and walking across the room. She opened the door and stepped into the hallway without a second thought. She moved to Landyn's door and reached for the handle.

Then stopped. What if he didn't want her?

Suddenly, the door swung open, and he stood there, shirtless. The light from the hallway washed over him, shading him in dark and light. Her mouth became moist, and she found it difficult to breathe.

They stared at each other for a long moment. Words escaped her. She could only stand before him helplessly, breathlessly, and feast on the sight of his magnificent torso and his beckoning lips.

He grabbed her wrist and yanked her into his room, pulling her into his embrace and lowering his mouth to hers in urgency. He kicked the door closed.

His body was fiery and hard as he pressed her against the wall to deepen the kiss.

She had not even paused to put on her armor or braid her hair. She'd come to him in her chemise, her hair wild about her shoulders. But it didn't matter. The only thing that mattered was feeling. Feeling him, feeling his touch.

He captured her head in his hands and moved his mouth over hers until she parted her lips, and he thrust his tongue forward, sweeping into her mouth, tasting her.

Shivers of desire shot through her body as his tongue explored the recesses of her mouth. Her knees weakened, and she clung to him, an anchor in her swirling world. His shoulders were sturdy and hot beneath her hands.

He trailed kisses along her lips and down her jaw to the base of her throat.

Instinctively, she tilted her head back, exposing her neck to him with an open-mouthed gasp. Her skin flamed beneath his mouth, coming to life with sensations she had never known.

His hands skimmed the sides of her body to the hem of her chemise. He dipped his hand beneath her garment to her bottom and stroked her rounded skin reverently.

An intense need consumed her. The chemise was in the way of feeling him—it was inhibiting her—and she arched her body into him as she lifted the fabric over her head and tossed it aside.

He took a moment to appraise her body with a heated stare.

Her breathing came in ragged gasps, and she reached eagerly for him. He pulled her against him, claiming her lips again with desperate heat.

The tips of her breasts met the firmness of his chest. He was hot and demanding, and she couldn't focus on anything but her need for him. She wanted him.

His fingers glided over her hips and squeezed her buttocks, pulling her against his hardness. She gasped as he brushed her core.

The sleek caress of his body made her moist with wanting. She pushed him back from her and reached for the strings of his leggings and tugged them open. She shoved them down over his legs, and his manhood sprang free.

Her eyes widened. Willow had told her about this, but she could never have imagined. She touched the tip, marveling at the way he responded with a heady groan.

He imprisoned her against him, capturing her lips in a searing kiss that sent flames through her veins. He turned her and backed her to the mattress, easing her back onto the blanket lying over the mattress. He held her protectively to him, skin to skin until they rested on the blanket. He lifted himself on one arm and trailed a passionate path of kisses to her chest.

She exhaled at the wondrous sensation his lips elicited. Her body was on fire, yet goosebumps covered her skin.

His fingers outlined the tip of her breast until her nipple was marble hard. Then, he lowered his mouth to it, kissing the sensitive tip and teasing it with his tongue.

She arched into his caress, passion pounding through her heart and mind. Her arms wrapped around his head as he laid his hard body atop of her.

He raised his head, his dark eyes smoldering as he pressed kisses across her collarbone, settling himself between her legs.

She opened her legs wider, and he fit against her hot core maddeningly well. Desire swirled through her, and their legs entwined. She felt him against the spot she needed him, the spot her body craved him. "Landyn," she gasped.

"Easy," he whispered. He held himself up on two hands on either side of her head.

She groaned in protest as their bodies separated, and she reached for him, resting her hands on his hips, gazing down at his magnificent torso.

He slid forward, his manhood filling her.

She inhaled a gasp as passion radiated into her body.

He held still for a moment before starting to move. Slowly, at first, pulling out and pushing forward.

Fiery heat radiated from her soft core, and she began to lift her hips, meeting his thrusts.

The tempo of their lovemaking increased, and their bodies met, one in rhythm.

Raven couldn't think rationally. They were in harmony together, and she soared higher and higher to a dimension where only she and Landyn existed. The world spun, elevating her higher and higher until finally, a glittering sensation of light and ecstasy exploded within her, sweeping her into its brilliance.

Landyn's body tightened at the same moment, and he pulled out, stroking his manhood. He splashed his seed across her stomach.

Raven blinked, much too sated and exhausted to acknowledge what he had done.

He took the blanket and wiped his seed from her stomach before settling beside her and gathering her into his arms. He kissed her forehead, and she grinned against his neck. She sighed and slipped into a satisfied slumber.

Landyn rose early, being careful not to wake Raven. She needed the sleep. As he separated himself from beside her, the scent of roses wafted to him from her hair, and he grinned, recalling the jar he'd caught her with at the stream. As he dressed and then sat on the floor to pull on his boots, he cast a glance back at her. She lay on the straw mattress, sleeping peacefully. Her long lashes rested against her cheeks, and her full lips were slightly parted. His heart swelled.

He loved her. There was nothing he was more certain of. He would do anything for her. But right now, he had to free the mercenary. He stood and departed the room quietly, pausing to tell Rolf where he was going in case Raven woke.

When he returned, he stood outside, staring over the grassy field toward the rising sun.

It was the most difficult decision of his life and yet the easiest. He knew what he was going to do. The Templars had saved him. John had saved him. And now, Landyn knew he would return the favor by saving Raven. He stood that way until the cock crowed, and he heard the inn door open behind him.

"Are you going to leave again?"

He turned to look at Raven as she exited the inn. She had donned her armor and braided her hair. She wore a fierce scowl of disapproval on her brow. And still, she was the most beautiful woman he had ever seen. For a moment, he was captivated by the slight sway of her hips.

She stopped before him, her hands on her waist. "I think I have a right to a goodbye."

He stared down at her thinned lips, and he knew he had made the right decision. But it had been difficult. "You do," Landyn admitted, turning to watch the bright rays of the sun peek over the horizon. "I have two vows, and I cannot possibly keep them both."

Her intense gaze was focused on his face.

He could feel her stare, as hot as the sun, and felt compelled to explain. "My oath to the Templars."

She stood, listening, not moving.

"And my oath to John."

Her hands dropped. "Landyn," she whispered, her voice softening in understanding.

"It is not a decision I take lightly."

"You don't have to do this," Raven said. "I'm sure my father would understand."

He faced her, his gaze moving tenderly over her and coming to rest on her irresistible lips. "It's more than just my oath to John. Or the Templars."

"You can't forsake your oath to the Templars," Raven argued. "They won't allow you to leave the order."

Landyn sighed gently. "I have not accepted the Holy Orders. I am as John was. A lay brother. We live and fight as Templars but have not taken the oath. I had always planned to." His voice turned wistful. "I had always planned to. And now…" He brushed a strand of her dark hair from her cheek. "I can't."

"You can still become a Templar," she protested. "You don't have to give up your dream."

"I can no longer become a Templar," he insisted.

Raven stepped away from him. "Is it because of what we did? Is it your vow of chastity?"

"No," he said, following her retreat. "I was never meant for a life of chastity. I realize that now."

"Then what?" Raven asked, her brow twisting with concern. "Don't give up your dream of becoming a Templar as my father did."

"For me, the Templars were a temporary oasis. A refuge from Boucher. A path to…" He took her shoulders and drew her to him. "You. You are my dream now."

She blinked, stunned.

"You are strong and honorable, confident and resourceful."

She blushed and bowed her head. "And excellent with a sword."

Laughter rumbled through him. "Aye. Excellent with a sword. And so very much more." He hooked his finger beneath her chin and lifted it to meet her gaze. "I was not going to leave. I gave you my word I would not, and I never will."

"Never?" she doubted, her eyebrows rising.

"Never," he promised, holding her against him.

She cocked her head to the side playfully while entwining her arms around him. "What if you find out that I snore?"

"I already know you do."

Her mouth dropped in mock insult. Then it snapped shut, and her chin tilted up. "What if you find out that I can't farm?"

"I am not looking for a farmer."

She sighed softly, melting against him. "What if you find out I am not the woman you *are* looking for?"

"You are unlike any other woman I've ever known. You have proven yourself to be more honorable and compassionate than anyone I've met. You are stunningly beautiful and talented and…" He couldn't resist. He pressed his lips to hers, covering any more objections. She was soft and passionate and thrilling and irresistible. He pulled back to look into her lidded eyes. "And I love you, Raven. I've fallen completely in love with you."

"You have?" she asked hopefully.

"Aye," he replied with a small grin.

"I love you, too, Landyn," she admitted, placing a warm hand against his cheek. "I think I've loved you for longer than I even knew." She inhaled deeply and lowered her hand. "Then, it is settled. We will find Sage and Willow, and you will marry me."

Landyn laughed out loud, throwing his head back. His joy surged to the heavens.

She gently hit his arm. "Isn't that what men and women who are in love do?"

"Aye," Landyn agreed tenderly. "It is."

CHAPTER NINETEEN

Raven rode down the dirt road beside Landyn. Open fields of swaying grass lined their path. She still couldn't believe Landyn loved her. She had never imagined being in love. She had prioritized the steel of a blade, the skill of fighting. Love wasn't something that had been important to her. Now, she wondered how that could ever have been.

She glanced at Landyn. His chin was lifted, and his eyes scanned the horizon. Just gazing at him set her heart pounding. She turned back to the road, adjusting her grip on the reins.

It was hard to fathom that such an amazing man, so decent and confident, could have fallen in love with a woman like her. He belonged with a lady of startling beauty who lived in a castle and wore rich garments. She shifted to ask him if he was certain he was in love with her.

His stare was focused on her, and he regarded her with such an intense, adoring expression that she blushed. And she knew. He did indeed love her.

"I suppose I lied," she admitted, recalling her earlier promise to him.

"Lied?" he repeated in confusion.

"I *did* fall in love with you after all."

He inhaled deeply and returned his attention to the road. "I should have warned you."

"Warned me about what?"

"That it would be difficult *not* to fall in love with me." A teasing smile stretched across his lips.

She matched his grin with one of her own.

"Tell me again where we are headed," Landyn said.

Raven nodded. "To Sybil's farm." She was grateful their father had the wisdom to plan a place to meet if they got separated. "We'll pass by Les Labadous and head to le Carla. I know a farmer there who will stock our supplies so we can continue south to Sybil's."

Landyn's eyebrows rose. "You certainly have everything figured out."

"You and I agreed to this path before we left the inn," she explained.

He lowered his chin and gazed at her with a heated look. "I like a woman who takes charge."

Her lower stomach flipped at his sultry stare, but she tried to console him. "We are partners. We worked this out together."

"It was a compliment," he asserted softly.

"Oh," she said, bowing her head in embarrassment. "I'm not used to them."

"You should start to get used to them. I plan to heap compliments on you every day," he said confidently. "You deserve them."

She lifted her chin proudly. She cast him a

sideways glance of admiration.

They traveled the entire day, stopping once to rest the horses and make love beneath a canopied forest.

When they came to the outskirts of Les Labadous, darkness had descended, and the moon was rising.

Raven was about to dismount when she noticed a trail of gray smoke curving against the black sky. She pointed it out to Landyn. "Something's burning," she observed uneasily. It looked too big to be a campfire.

"Someone might need help," Landyn said, his horse dancing nervously beneath him.

She nodded. Given the direction, it looked as if a building were burning in Les Labadous. The blaze was not under control, and the owners likely needed aid fighting it. She spurred her steed into a trot, following the clouds. They charged across harvested farmers' fields, mud kicking up in their wake.

As they moved closer, the fire reached toward the night sky like fingers, trying to grasp at the stars. A barn at the edge of the farmers' fields burned, the flames snapping and crackling with tongues of heat.

A forest lined the fields. Raven dismounted close to the trees, so the animals didn't get frightened by the fire. She and Landyn tethered them to a tree branch and hurried toward the barn.

No one was attempting to extinguish the fire; no one had even come to watch. Confused, she slowed to a walk.

"It looks abandoned," Landyn observed.

Through one of the loose planks of the wall, Raven saw a shadow shift inside. "There's someone in there." Just as she reached the door, it was shoved open.

A shadow emerged, cast in darkness from the hungry, red fire engulfing the barn behind.

Raven drew her sword, preparing to fight. Then she froze. Recognition drained through her as the shadow's hand dropped to the pommel of her sword.

A man moved protectively forward behind the silhouette.

Raven's chest constricted. She knew every aspect of the woman standing before her. Her armor, her movements, her outline.

Sage!

"Raven," the woman gasped.

Raven tossed her sword aside, and the two women lurched to embrace each other tightly. Raven clung to Sage, squeezing her with relief and elation. She never wanted to let her go.

Sage buried her face in Raven's shoulder.

She smelled of burning ash. But it didn't matter. It was Sage. Here. Raven hugged her tightly for a long moment before pulling away. Her gaze brushed over her sister's face with concern.

"Are you well?" both asked at the same time.

Each let out a relieved chuckle.

Raven's stare swept over Sage. She seemed unhurt. But her brown hair was different. Raven frowned. Sage's long hair was gone, replaced by shoulder-length locks. "What happened to your hair?"

Behind them, a beam collapsed with a snap, sending embers spiraling into the air.

Raven cringed as a sweltering hot blast of air swept out from the barn to surround them.

The blond-haired man in the barn with Sage put an arm around her waist and guided her away from the building, locking gazes with Raven.

Raven's protective instincts took over, and she set her jaw stiffly. Who was this man, and why was he touching Sage? More importantly, why was Sage letting him?

Sage clasped Raven's hand and tugged her with them.

Raven cast a glance behind them to see Landyn retrieve her sword from the ground and follow. As she turned back to Sage, her stare lingered on the man's familiar hold on her younger sister. He wore clothing that didn't seem to fit him. His brown tunic was tight around his shoulders. If he moved his arms, it might rip.

What had occurred in the five days that they had been separated? How had this man and Sage gotten so close, so quickly? Then she glanced at Landyn. It had happened to her. How could she fault Sage?

Raven released Sage's hand, and Landyn handed her sword to her. She sheathed it.

They traipsed through the harvested field to the forest line where two horses were tethered. The horses were only a hundred paces from Raven and Landyn's horses. Raven wondered how she had missed them.

Sage stopped beside her horse. She glanced at Raven with a grin.

Raven was happy she had found her sister and answered with a smile of her own. Her contentment faded as she glanced at the field and forest around them. "Where's Willow?"

Sage's joy vanished. "She's not with you?"

"No," Raven explained with growing concern. "She disappeared in the Chateau le Bezu. I thought she was right behind me, but she wasn't." Seeing the worry in Sage's eyes, she assured her, "We'll find her."

A large crash sounded from the barn, drawing Raven's attention. The fire consumed the structure, sizzling and snapping as angry red flames stretched into the sky. Thick gray smoke rolled from the interior of the burning structure.

It wouldn't be long before the villagers arrived.

"We should leave here," the man with Sage suggested, staring at the barn.

Raven glared at him. So many questions raced through her mind.

Sage nodded and took his hand into her own. She looked at Raven. "I want you to meet Marcus." She turned to him and introduced, "This is my sister, Raven."

Raven greeted him with a curt nod, still not satisfied. She wanted details. Where had they met? Her gaze dropped to their entwined fingers. And what was their relationship?

Landyn stood beside Raven. "This is Sir Landyn," she said. But Raven couldn't take her gaze from Marcus. Her stare pinned him, trying to sum him up. His lip was swollen as if he had been in a fight, and he was holding his side as though he were injured. She scanned her sister, but she seemed unhurt. "Are you in trouble?"

Sage shrugged and grinned helplessly. "Always. The king's man, Nogaret, is looking for us."

Raven's mouth dropped and then closed into a thin line of displeasure. She shook her head. The king? she thought. Of anyone to make angry, the king was not the one.

"He's looking for a book Sage decoded," Marcus clarified with pride in his voice.

"A book?" Raven wondered. "The book we brought to Brother Nicolas?"

Sage nodded.

"Why is he looking for it? What's inside?"

"Directions," Sage answered. "To what, we aren't sure."

They quickly left Les Labadous and rode for half the night until Sage insisted that they stop so she could treat Marcus's wounds.

Sheltered off the road, under tall trees that swayed beneath a soft breeze, the group rested.

Raven sat beside Landyn below one of the thin tree trunks. Dappled moonlight rained down upon them, making it light enough that she could see Sage ministering to a shirtless Marcus near a small stream. "I can't believe we found her," she whispered with relief. "If only we could find Willow so easily."

Landyn took her hand into his own, pressing a kiss to her knuckles. "We'll find her."

Raven relaxed slightly against his shoulder, a

blush spreading across her cheeks. Even Landyn's words did not relax the stirrings of unease and concern for Willow. "We'll head to Sybil's farm and…" Her words trailed off as her nervousness rose.

"She'll be there," Landyn insisted. He glanced at Sage and Marcus.

Raven followed his gaze. They were speaking quietly. Sage leaned into Marcus, happy and content. Happier than Raven had ever seen her. When Marcus wrapped his arms around Sage and pulled her close to kiss her, Raven straightened, feeling an instant surge of protectiveness.

Landyn chuckled softly, drawing Raven's glare. "What's so funny?" she demanded.

"Your reaction to them. I wonder if your sister feels the same about us."

Raven sighed and settled against Landyn. Even though Sage was her little sister, she was a grown woman capable of making her own choices. Raven still had many questions, but she would wait until Sage was ready to tell her story. "She must love him," Raven said softly. "Sage would never allow a man to kiss her."

"Maybe she pushed him down first," Landyn said softly with a playful grin.

Raven stared at Landyn with a grin. "That is reserved for me. Sage probably would have hit him over the head with a book."

They shared a quiet smile before Raven stroked his arm affectionately. Her body came alive with the touch, and her glance trailed to his lips. Riding with Sage was going to test her restraint with Landyn. It was strange how a week could have changed their lives so much.

Sage stepped away from Marcus and sat in an open grassy area awash in moonlight. She pulled out parchment pages from her boot and spread them on the ground.

"This book that Sage is so interested in," Landyn said, watching Sage's movements. "Where did she get it?"

Raven shrugged. "First, Willow claimed she found it. But later, she told Brother Nicolas it was a gift. I'm not really sure where she got it."

Landyn shook his head. "I don't like this. Even if it is directions, the book was coded. It means there is something that we were not meant to find."

"It's a mystery. Sage loves mysteries," Raven admitted.

"Still, if Nogaret is after the book…"

"You know Nogaret?" she asked, surprised.

"I know *of* him. He is the king's man. We must be cautious."

Landyn observed Sage work. She placed the parchment pages carefully before her, flattening them with her hand, and attempted to decode them. His gaze shifted to Marcus. He had seen him before. When Marcus strolled toward the horses, Landyn rose and followed. When he came near Marcus, he planted his feet and crossed his arms. "I saw you at le Bezu."

"I was there," Marcus admitted while reaching into the saddlebag to remove a flask. "I trained there for a bit." He uncorked the flask and drank deeply.

"I saw you a week ago, just before Brother Nicolas was found dead," Landyn said, being careful to keep the condemnation from his voice. This man was important to Raven's sister. Landyn didn't want to create trouble.

Marcus lowered the flask from his lips and wiped a sleeve across his mouth. "Are you accusing me?"

"It is suspicious, don't you think?"

Marcus shifted his gaze to Raven and back to Landyn. "Aren't you a Templar knight?"

Landyn straightened, his eyes narrowing. He was close to being a Templar. That was all Marcus needed to know. "I was."

"I've finished!" Sage cried.

Landyn glanced over his shoulder at Sage.

Marcus placed the cork back on the flask, returned it to the saddlebag, and hurried to Sage's side. Landyn followed.

Raven stood over Sage, gazing down at the parchment pages as they shone in the moonlight.

Marcus dropped to his knees at Sage's side. "Where do the directions lead?" he asked breathlessly.

Sage shook her head, rubbing a hand over her chin in confusion. "I don't know."

"Doesn't it say in the book?" Marcus asked.

"No. It doesn't say anything except the directions. It doesn't even say where to start, and there is no specific end."

Landyn scowled. All directions had a starting point. Otherwise, how could they follow them? Had she read them properly?

Marcus stared. "There's nowhere to start?"

"What kind of directions are those?" Raven asked incredulously.

"The kind that wants to stay hidden," Landyn stated. "We were not meant to know what the directions were for."

Sage sat back on her heels and crossed her arms. "I don't believe that. There must be more. Something we're missing."

Tingles of forewarning danced across Landyn's nape. There was something about this book that set his nerves on edge.

Crickets chirped in the clearing beside the forest.

Marcus glanced toward the field. He stood, taking hold of Sage's arm and helping her to her feet. "We can think about this later. We should leave here."

"Maybe we should go back to le Bezu," Sage suggested, bending to gather up the parchment pages. "We have to find Willow."

"Sybil's farm. We were to meet there if we ever got separated," Raven reminded them.

Sage agreed with a nod as she tucked the parchment into her boot. She picked up the quill and ink and looked at her sister, cocking her head. "How did you get here? How did you find me?"

Raven exchanged a look with Landyn. "It's a long story. I'll tell you on the way."

CHAPTER TWENTY

On the ride to Sybil's farm, Raven told Sage all about her and Landyn's journey — Boucher's cruelties, the empty crates, and the key father had given her. But she couldn't bring herself to disclose that Father was gone. She wanted to wait and tell her sisters when they were together, mostly for selfish reasons. She didn't want to have to relive it again. When Sage asked where Father was, Raven told her he had something to take care of. He always had some job to do, so Sage didn't question her father's absence.

As the sun began to rise, Sage relayed her story. She said she had met Marcus in the chateau, and they departed together.

"You left us there?" Raven asked in anger. "You left without finding us?"

"It was on my insistence," Marcus said, defending Sage.

Raven swung her gaze to Marcus with a scowl

of disapproval.

"We couldn't wait," Sage clarified.

That didn't appease Raven. "You could have found us and told us."

Sage glanced at Marcus. "Marcus promised to teach me to read. And he did! I can read now."

It was as though Sage and Raven were from two unrelated countries. Different things were important to them. "I was worried about you."

"I'm sorry," Sage answered sincerely.

Raven sighed softly. She loved Sage, even though Sage didn't make the most rational decisions. "I'm happy you can read."

Sage grinned at Raven, pleased and surprised at the admission.

"Then you don't know that Brother Nicolas was murdered," Landyn explained.

Raven noted there was something in his voice, some underlying tone. It was as though he were trying to judge their reaction.

Sage nodded. "I know." She looked at Marcus. "We were there. That's why I had to go with Marcus."

"If you were there, who killed him?"

"I don't know," Sage said quickly.

Raven met Landyn's gaze. Sage wasn't telling the truth. Raven knew her sister and could tell she was keeping something from them. It looked as if they both had secrets.

Sage continued her story.

Finally, when the sun was high overhead, they arrived at the small village of le Val. It was nestled between two hills in a valley. Sybil's farm was the last structure on the south side of the town.

They went around the hills of the small village, so no one knew they were there. The location was one of the reasons their father liked the farm so much. That, and Sybil's friendship.

They rounded one of the grassy mounds, and the single-story wooden structure came into view. Three fields surrounded the building, two harvested and empty. One was filled with stalks of barley.

Raven felt a twinge of guilt. She should have been there to help Sybil with the harvest. She knew it was a lot of work for the women.

Her gaze shifted to the cottage, and a warm feeling of comfort and safety spread through her. Her family travelled around a lot. Sybil's farm was the closest place to a home they had. They could rest here and feel secure. She slid from the saddle.

While the others dismounted, she scanned the fields. Anxiety swelled within her. Where was Willow? She couldn't see her friends, either. Maybe they were all inside the cottage. Finally, she took up Thunder's reins and began walking down the dirt path.

A small breeze rushed by, stirring fallen leaves around her feet.

Amid the stalks of barley in a field, she spotted a dark head poke up. A young girl watched them for a moment before running toward the cottage.

Raven grinned. She recognized Emma immediately by her slight limp. The girl had fallen from a tree when she was young and injured her leg. It had never healed correctly.

Landyn moved up beside her. She inhaled a deep breath and cast him a nervous glance. She wished it had been Willow's blonde head she saw amidst the barley stalks.

Landyn reached out to caress her hand. She wrapped her fingers around his, finding reassurance in his touch.

Emma disappeared into the cottage, leaving the door open as they approached.

After a moment, another woman emerged. Her dark hair was tied in a bun. She held a hand to her forehead to block the sunlight as she watched them approach.

Raven smiled. Vivian was Sybil's daughter.

As they neared, Vivian lowered her hand to reveal a huge smile. She spoke to Emma.

Emma squealed in delight and rushed toward them.

Behind Raven, Sage grunted. Raven turned to see Cassie embracing her sister from behind. Cassie was just a year younger than Emma's twelve summers. Her brown hair was in wild disarray around her shoulders, and her arms were locked around Sage's neck.

Raven held out her arms as Emma launched herself toward her. She caught her with an exhalation of air. "You're getting big," she commented, hugging the girl tightly.

"Are you staying long?" Cassie asked in an excited voice.

"Who are they?" Emma wondered, looking curiously at Landyn and Marcus.

"Emma loves a boy," Cassie tattled.

"I do not!" Emma replied, scowling.

Raven cast Sage a weary but happy glance. The girls had incessant questions, but they never waited for answers. It was always good to see them.

Raven handed Emma Thunder's reins. "Can you both take care of the horses for us? They've had a long trip."

Emma and Cassie nodded enthusiastically, each girl taking two horses and leading them toward a field on the side of the cottage.

Raven strolled up to the cottage, where Vivian waited with her hands on her hips. "You are late," she said with mock sternness.

"Leave 'em alone, Viv!" a voice called from inside.

"Well, come in," Vivian said, standing aside to let them into the cottage. She eyed the men as they passed.

Landyn nodded a greeting to her.

Marcus looked over his shoulder at the horses.

The cottage was large compared with others. A table was positioned in the center of the room, surrounded by four chairs. There was another door in the corner of the room that led to the sleeping chambers. All four slept in the same room. A hearth with a warm fire was on the wall farthest from the doorway. An elderly woman with gray hair twisted in her chair near the small fire in the hearth so that she could see the door.

A smile erupted over Raven's lips, and she hurried in to embrace her. Sybil. Sage followed, hugging the old woman.

"It's good to see you girls," Sybil said softly. The fire lit her from behind, casting an orange glow over her wrinkled skin.

Raven inhaled. Her cottage always smelled of lavender and a piney, floral scent.

"And who are these men?" Vivian demanded

sternly.

Sage introduced them. "This is Marcus and Landyn."

Vivian shook her head. "Your father would not be pleased."

"I am John's friend," Landyn said. "He tasked me with seeing to Raven's safety."

Raven rolled her eyes.

"Is that true?" Sage asked.

Raven nodded and shrugged. "You know Father." She knew she would have to tell all of them the truth about Father. The thought sent a wave of sadness through her, and she bowed her head.

Sybil's shrewd gaze assessed Marcus and Landyn.

"Since you're so late, we certainly can use extra hands for the harvest," Vivian proclaimed.

Raven agreed. "Of course, we'll help."

Sage knelt beside Sybil, wrapping her curved fingers with her hand. "Sybil. Is Willow here?"

Sybil furrowed her brow in confusion. "She didn't come with you?"

"I assumed she went with Emma and Cassie," Vivian explained, her worried stare shifting from Sage to Raven.

Willow wasn't there. Trepidation snaked up Raven's spine. Was Willow hurt? Where was she? She couldn't lose both her father and her sister. She couldn't.

Landyn stepped up to her and dipped his head to catch her focus. "We'll find her," he promised.

But Raven didn't know where else to look. Concern filled her. She wanted to feel Landyn's warm embrace, his comforting touch. Instead, she looked at Sage.

Her sister's brow was creased with worry. She gently bit her lower lip.

Where was Willow?

Find out where Willow is! Read Willow's story.

Sneak Peek
Willow

PROLOGUE

1304
In a field in France

"𝔜ou think you can disarm me?"

His voice made Willow smile. She knew Christian well enough to know that he was taunting her into a foolish move. Willow stared at him; her sword held before her. He was so handsome with those blue eyes twinkling beneath the hot summer sun. His strong, square jaw dripped with perspiration from their workout. Yet, even beneath the warm sun, his sword arm was sure, the tip of his blade pointed directly at her heart. "With but a smile, Sir."

"I'm no knight and you know it," he said and swung his sword at her.

She had purposely goaded him into a reckless move, and she caught his sword with her own, twisting her wrist. Normally, the move would have been good enough to fling his sword out of his grip and send it flying through the air. But this was Christian. And he was good. Very good.

He smiled. "Very good, Willow. You almost had me."

"Almost," she repeated without letting her disappointment show. Slowly, she stepped around him keeping her sword tip between them. "Father would say almost doesn't win a battle."

"And he would be correct." Christian matched her steps, keeping the swords between them.

"Where is Father?"

"He is looking for work in town."

Father was always looking for work. It took a lot to support his three daughters. But he had not lacked. Not in the twelve years she had been with him. Not since their mother died. "Why aren't you looking for work?"

"*You* are my work."

She swung and connected with his blade. "I should find that insulting." The blow clanged through the small glade where they practiced. "I am most certainly not work!" But his comment had insulted her. As the youngest sister, she had always sought to keep up with her sisters. Raven was a natural with the sword. And Sage was brilliant. She could figure out how anything worked.

Christian attacked, swinging his sword again and again, driving her backward. He arced the blade over her head, and she put hers up to block it. He caught her sword, flicked his wrist and sent her blade flying. "That's how it's done."

Willow scowled at Christian. "You better not

have lost my blade."

"Me? I believe it came out of your hand," he said, following her across the glade into a thick patch of long grass where the blade had flown to.

Willow stood at the edge of the long grass. "We'll never find it."

He sheathed his weapon. "Not standing here, we won't." He marched passed her into the grass and it swallowed him, closing the path behind him.

Willow could still make out the direction he had gone from the bent stalks. She started in a different direction. If she could find it first, she would still win. She started kicking the stalks, searching the ground. The long stems moved, but they were so thick she might easily miss her sword. She fell to her knees and used her hands, pushing the stems, feeling the ground. Back and forth in a systematic pattern. She would not miss it. And she would find it first.

She crawled forward when she had cleared an area. Still searching. Swinging her hand in a semi-circle before her. Back and forth. Then the other hand. Back and forth. She was so hot beneath the bright rays of the sun and from practicing and now from searching. Back and forth. What if she didn't find it? Father would be furious. They couldn't afford another sword.

Christian suddenly appeared on his hands and knees, searching as she was. His hand brushed hers. And froze.

Their eyes met. Her heart leapt, but it had nothing to do with her exertion. "I'm never going to find it," she whispered.

He leaned toward her. "You will."

Her gaze dipped to his lips and then quickly back to his beautiful blue eyes. He was close to her. Closer than when he started out. His warm hand on top of hers sent waves of hot tingles through her body. He reached for her with his other hand and the next thing she knew, he pressed his lips to hers. Warmth flooded through her body in response to the pressure of his gentle lips. They moved over hers with a soft, sensual caress.

The world was swept out from beneath her, swirling. It was as if she were floating.

He pulled back to look into her eyes.

All she could think of was... Christian. Her gaze swept his face, his ruggedly handsome strong face, to his moist lips. She had wanted to kiss him, to know what he felt like. But she had been unprepared for the emotions flaring to life inside her. Confusion, doubt, arousal, excitement. She parted her lips to speak, but no words came out.

In unison, they came forward into each other's arms, kneeling. Their bodies pressed together; their arms went around each other. Their kiss deepened, putting all the passion and unhindered longing into their touch.

Willow's mind spun, with every heated touch of his lips, with every stroke of his masterful tongue.

"Willow!"

Willow separated instantly. Father! She whirled to find him standing behind them. His dark gaze moved from her to Christian and back. Willow stood. "My sword." She looked at the ground, as if looking for her weapon. "I was searching for it."

Her father said nothing for a long moment.

Willow lifted her gaze to him.

He stared at her with an intense gaze. "You lost it?"

She swallowed as her cheeks flamed.

"It was my fault, John," Christian said, stepping to Willow's side. "We were practicing, and I disarmed her."

John's look darkened, his brows slanting over his eyes as he looked at Christian.

"We'll find it," Christian promised.

"Willow, return to camp," her father ordered.

"My sword," she said softly.

"If you lost it, you don't deserve to own it."

At his hard tone, a stab of remorse filled her. She bobbed her head. "Yes, Father." She raced back to the camp.

Willow combed down her mare, Mercy. She put all her heart into taking care of what was hers. She knew they didn't have a lot of coin, so when her father entrusted something to her, she knew she had to care for it. Her father had given her Mercy five summers ago. The sword he had given to her on her six summers ago. She had never lost it before.

Strangely, her mind continued to return to Christian's kiss. She replayed it over and over in her mind. He had kissed her! It had been wondrously delicious. His lips had been so much more then she imagined. She ran her tongue over her lips, but no matter how she tried, she could not repeat the sensations his lips had elicited.

Caught between guilt and wonderment, Willow saw her father marching back into camp. He was carrying her sword! Joy erupted through her. "You found it!" She crossed to him, and he tossed it to her.

"Aye," he said. "Don't lose it again."

Willow inspected the blade. It needed to be cleaned and she would take care of it. Slowly, she lowered the blade. Her father moved passed her. "Where's Christian?"

"He left." There was a finality to his voice.

Left. She couldn't help the feeling of rejection surging within her. "When will he be back?"

"Put him out of your mind," her father ordered.

Willow looked back at the thick forest. How could she possibly do that now? "Where did he go?"

"He said something about a pressing matter. He's not coming back, Willow." He continued on to the smoldering fire in the center of the camp.

Willow's heart twisted. Those were the same words he had said about her mother. She had driven Christian away. Not good enough. Never good enough.

She sheathed her weapon and turned to her horse. She would never leave her. The horse nickered softly, and she wrapped her arms around the mare's neck. She closed her eyes. Why would he leave her?

ENJOY THIS BOOK? I COULD USE YOUR HELP

Reviews are the most powerful tools I have to get attention for my books. Just a simple sentence or two of why you enjoyed it would help other medieval romance fans find my books. I would really appreciate a moment of your time and an honest review!

Thank you!

ABOUT THE AUTHOR

Critically acclaimed and bestselling author Laurel O'Donnell has won numerous awards for her works, including the Holt Medallion for A Knight of Honor, the Happily Ever After contest for Angel's Assassin, and the Indiana's Golden Opportunity contest for Immortal Death. The Angel and the Prince was nominated by the Romance Writers of America for their prestigious Golden Heart award.

When not writing, you can often find her lounging with her five cats or researching ideas online for the next book. She loves to visit the Renaissance Faire, spend time with family and hear from her readers.

She finds precious time every day to escape into the medieval world and bring her characters to life in her writing.

Subscribe to her newsletter so you don't miss out on upcoming new releases and fun contests. http://bit.ly/laurel-odonnell

Thank you for reading!